SKELETON KEYS

THE
WILD IMAGININGS
OF STANLEY STRANGE

WRITTEN BY
GUY BASS

ILLUSTRATED BY
PETE WILLIAMSON

LITTLE TIGER
LONDON

The Key to
Reality

The Key to
Second Sight

The Key to
Doorminion

The Forbidden Key

The Key to Time

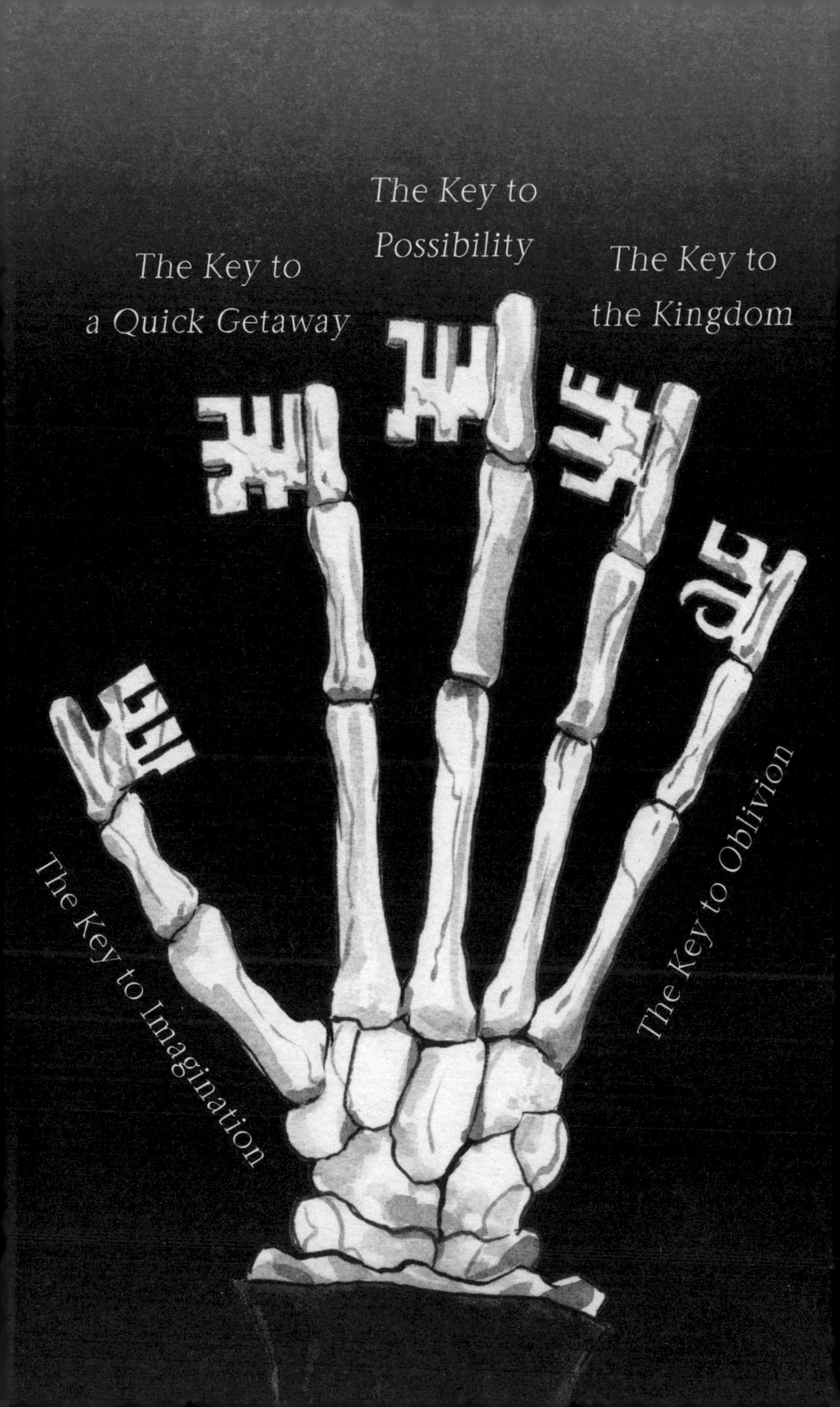
The Key to
Possibility
The Key to
a *Quick Getaway*
The Key to
the *Kingdom*
The Key to Imagination
The Key to Oblivion

Greetings! To pottlers, do-to-dos and fly-a-ways! To the imaginary and the unimaginary! To the living, the dead and everyone in between, my name is Keys ... Skeleton Keys.

A moon or more ago, before even your wrinkliest relatives were considering being born, I was an IF – an imaginary friend. Then, by a waft of wild imagining, I was suddenly as real as rabbits! I had become *unimaginary*.

Today, Ol' Mr Keys keeps a watchful eye socket on those IFs who have been recently *unimagined*. Wherever they appear, so do I! For these fantabulant fingers of mine open doors to anywhere and elsewhere ... hidden worlds ... secret places ... doors to the limitless realm of all imagination. And each door has led to an adventure and then some! The stories I could tell you...

Of course, that is why you are here – for

a *story*. Well, fret not! Here is a hum-dum-dinger of a tale to send your brain into a tailspin. A truly unbelievable, unbelievably true tale I can only call *The Wild Imaginings of Stanley Strange*.

Stanley imagined his IF five years ago, five days after his fifth birthday. He named him Lucky, and the pair of them have been best friends ever since. Stanley never goes anywhere without imagining Lucky – and Lucky wants nothing more than to be Stanley's favourite figment. Truth be told, Stanley and his IF are inseparable.

So then, how is it that Lucky suddenly finds himself as real as cheese and all alone? How can he be real if Stanley is nowhere to be found? How can an IF become unimaginary if there is no one there to unimagine him? I cannot imagine! But strange things can happen when *Strange* imaginations run wild...

Our story begins upon a hill. The night is dark and there is no shelter from the cold, cruel wind that batters and buffets the land. A lone figure wanders hither and thither, wondering how he came to be there and what became of the boy who imagined him...

CHAPTER ONE

LUCKY

(LOST AND FOUND)

"Every adventure begins with a step into the unknown."

—SK

"Stanley?"

Lucky's cry was lost to the whipping wind. All he could see were hills, stretching out across the far-reaching darkness. He wasn't sure how long he'd been out here, or how long Stanley had been gone. But most of all, why did everything feel so different ... so *real*? The wind was bitter and unkind and chilled him to the bone. Lucky had never felt anything like it. He called his friend's name again but Stanley was nowhere to be seen.

Plump sheep dotted the landscape, braced

against the wind. "Excuse me, have you seen Stanley?" he asked one of them but the sheep just gazed at him in bafflement. Indeed, Lucky was an odd-looking creature – no taller than the sheep itself, with stubby arms and legs and a covering of vivid orange velvety fur. His monkey-like face was bright blue, and black stripes covered a pouch on his belly. A bushy orange tail went all the way up from the small of his back to the top of his head.

"Have you seen Stanley?" Lucky asked another sheep. After quizzing three more, he rubbed his forehead and found a painful bruise as big as an egg. How did he get that? Lucky's mind raced with questions but one repeated over and over in his head.

Where's Stanley?

The wind seemed to push against him as he trudged across the hill. Then, after a moment, he spotted something – no – *someone*.

They were coming straight for him.

"Stanley...?" Lucky whispered, his voice swallowed by fear. "S-Stanley? Is that you?"

"*Boo,*" said a voice. Lucky froze as a figure stepped out of the fog-laden gloom.

It was a girl. She wore a striped dress and had pigtails in her hair, and everything about her was as grey as an old television show.

And her head was on back to front.

"Y-you're not Stanley..." Lucky whimpered, edging away.

"I'm *Daisy,* dummy," the girl said with a glower. "I can turn invisible. What can you do, except look like an orange?"

"Daisy! What have I told you about niggling the newly unimagined?" said another voice. From behind the backwards-headed girl emerged a far grimmer figure – a living skeleton in a tailored suit. He peered down at Lucky, eyeballs floating impossibly in his skull.

"Fret not, figment," said the skeleton, the words clattering out of his mouth. "You have nothing to fear from us."

"Speak for yourself," said the girl. She turned on Lucky. "We've been wandering around looking for you for hours, you tangerine."

"Daisy, do resist the urge to be yourself

for the moment," suggested the skeleton, before turning back to Lucky. "My name is Keys ... Skeleton Keys, and this is my partner-in-problem-solving, Daisy," he said. "Like you, we are inventions of imagination made suddenly, wildly *real*. We are unimaginary!"

"Unimagine-dairy?" Lucky said, trying to wrap his mouth around the word.

"Fantabulantly so!" replied Skeleton Keys. He tapped the side of his skull with his fingers and Lucky saw that each digit ended in a bone key. "And although Ol' Mr Keys was on the other side of elsewhere, I felt the *twitch*, that eerie rattling of my skull which told me that an IF had been unimagined. *You*, figment."

"I'm not sure I *want* to be unimagine-dairy. I feel all ... solid," said Lucky, poking his face with a furry finger. The thought of being out in the real world made him feel more lost than ever. He glanced up at Skeleton Keys and, not for the last time, asked, "Where's Stanley?"

"Stanley? Is that the ankle-sprout who imagined you?" replied the skeleton.

Lucky nodded, his eyes wet with tears. "His name's Stanley Strange," he said, wiping his nose with a furry forearm. "He's got glasses and a stripy hat and he's my biggin best friend in all the world."

"If he imagined you, he has a lot to answer for," Daisy grumbled.

"My twitch became most *itchy-twitchy* not three hours ago," Skeleton Keys explained to Lucky. "In that very moment, Stanley Strange must have imagined you so well that you suddenly became as real as elbows. Such is the wonder of wild imagining!"

"So, where is he?" Daisy asked, eyeing Lucky suspiciously. "Did you eat him?"

"What? No!" Lucky cried. He rubbed the bruise on his head. "I *saw* him. He was standing right in front of me ... and then he wasn't. Like he vanished!"

"Confuddlement is quite natural for the recently unimagined," explained Skeleton Keys. "Do you remember your name, figment?"

"Lucky," he replied, shivering against the cold. "I'm Lucky."

"Lost on a hill in the dark? Doesn't seem very lucky to me, *Stan-fan*," Daisy sneered.

"Stanley called me Lucky," said Lucky, swelling with pride despite Daisy's withering words. "Stanley likes eggs and *toast shoulders* and pretend karate and he can draw a proper robot in five minutes flat and ... where is he? Where's Stanley?"

Skeleton Keys pulled the collar of his jacket around his neck as the wind whistled in and out of his skull, and stared across the hill.

"That, little figment," he said, "is what we are going to find out."

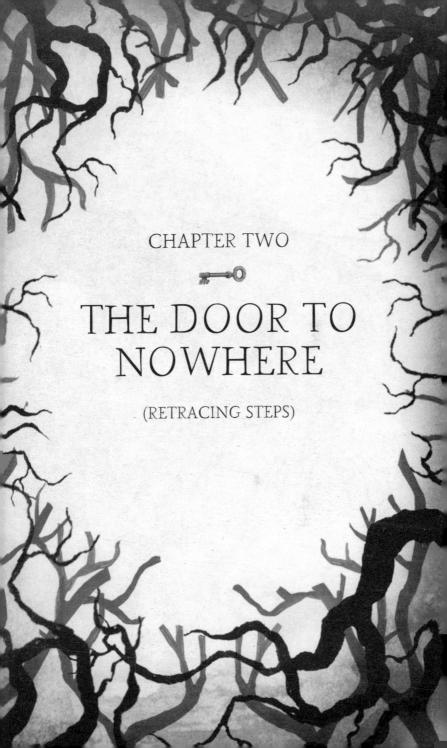

CHAPTER TWO

THE DOOR TO NOWHERE

(RETRACING STEPS)

*"A journey of a thousand wild imaginings
begins with a single thought."*
—SK

"Fret not, figment! Ol' Mr Keys will find
your friend," Skeleton Keys declared,
striding across the hill as if he was quite sure
which way to go. "Humans are an unpredictable
lot, but they cannot simply vanish."

"Stanley did!" Lucky replied, hopping
after the skeleton like a kangaroo. "I was all
snuggled and safe in the back of his mind –
my second-best place to be after the front of
his mind – then suddenly I was out here in
the dark and the cold, and there was Stanley!
But then he wasn't..."

"Maybe your 'friend' got sick of your constant yakking and left you here," Daisy grumbled, following huffily behind them.

"Not a chance in one million!" Lucky said. "Stanley says I'm his biggin best friend in the whole biggin world, even though I'm not real. Which I s'pose I am, now."

"Does Stanley ever tell you to shut your face?" Daisy tutted.

"Yep!" replied Lucky happily. "Stanley says I could talk the stripes off a tiger, which is his seventh favourite animal. One time I was saying all the flavours of crisps, one time I was counting clouds, one time I tried to say the alphabet backwards, one time I—"

"*Shut up,*" Daisy grunted and tried to catch up with Skeleton Keys. "Do we really have to find this mango's friend, bone-bag?"

"We help whomever *needs* us, Daisy," said the skeleton. He stopped in his tracks and spun towards Lucky. "Let us start by retracing your steps, figment. What is the first thing you remember *after* you were unimagined?"

"I-I'm not sure I remember the first thing I remember," Lucky began. "But I saw Stanley – at least I think I did. There was light … big and biggin bright and he was staring right at it. I ran towards him – ran towards the light – but then I banged my biggin head. By the time my brain had stopped being bumped, I was all on my own. No light … and no Stanley. I must have wandered off and got myself well and biggin lost."

"Ugh, just admit you ate him and we can all go home," Daisy said.

"What if he's lost forever and ever and ever and ever?" exclaimed Lucky in a sudden panic. "What if I never find him?"

"Perhaps we need to go back further – to *before* you were unimagined," suggested

Skeleton Keys. "Do you remember how Stanley came to be amble-rambling upon these hilltops?"

"Same reason he always comes here," replied Lucky. "Stanley wanted to see the door."

"What door?" huffed Daisy.

"The one at the top of the hill," replied Lucky. "The Door to Nowhere."

"Nowhere?" Skeleton Keys repeated. He froze, his unblinking eyes suddenly wider than ever. "A door to nowhere, figment? Are you certain?"

"Stanley goes biggin loads – he likes to doodle his doodles there," replied Lucky. "Stanley says he likes the Door to Nowhere 'cause it doesn't make sense. Why have a door that goes to nowhere?"

"Sticks 'n' stones, of course! How could I have been such a saddle-goose?" whispered Skeleton Keys, whirling around as if desperate to get his bearings. "In this confuddling gloom I did not realize where we were, but of course ... *this* is where I left it."

"Left what?" Daisy asked, eyeing the skeleton suspiciously. "Ugh, you look like you've just remembered that you did something stupid."

"Is it that-a-way?" the skeleton mused, holding up a single, key-tipped finger as if checking the direction of the wind. "No, this-a-way!"

Skeleton Keys suddenly broke into long strides. Lucky followed behind with bounding hops, while Daisy's awkward, backwards run left her lagging behind. Dawn light began to crest over the horizon as Skeleton Keys rounded the summit of the hill. As Lucky hurried alongside he saw a familiar silhouette, standing tall on the top of the hill.

A door.

It stood in its frame, solitary and strange, leading nowhere.

"That's it – that's biggin it!" he cried.

"What's it?" shouted Daisy as she struggled to keep up.

"The Door to Nowhere!" replied Lucky. "Mr Keys found it!"

"Found it, figment?" said Skeleton Keys with a glint in his eyeball. "I did a lot more than that – I *put* it there."

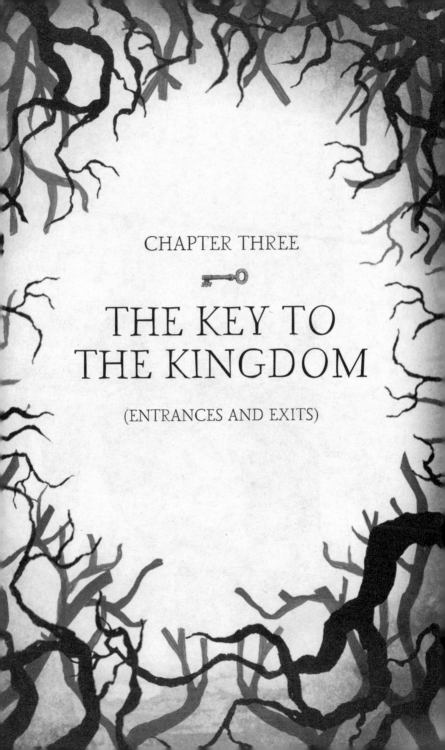

CHAPTER THREE

THE KEY TO
THE KINGDOM

(ENTRANCES AND EXITS)

My Kingdom for a Kingdom!

As the morning sun began its slow ascent over the horizon, Skeleton Keys, Daisy and Lucky gathered around the simple wooden door. It stood, lonely and absurd, on the top of the hill.

"Daisy, it's the Door to Nowhere!" said Lucky giddily. "This is where Stanley was going!"

He raced around the door once, twice and a third time, hoping to somehow find Stanley on the other side ... but his best friend was nowhere to be seen.

"You are exactly as dumb as you look, you

mango," Daisy puffed as Lucky slowed to a disappointed halt. She spotted something on the ground a few paces from the door and bent down to pick it up. It was a sketchbook, dog-eared and slightly battered. On the cover was a name, written in capital letters – STANLEY. Daisy started flicking through the pages, to find them crammed with carefully crafted sketches. The first half of the book mainly featured bees, but on later pages Daisy found fierce dinosaurs, rampaging robots and alien invaders from far-off worlds. "What's this?" she huffed.

"Stanley's doodle diary!" cried Lucky, hopping over to her. "He never goes nowhere without his doodle diary..."

"'Doodle diary'? Eww," said Daisy with a grimace. She tossed the book at Lucky, who immediately checked to make sure all the pages were intact.

"Stanley's always doodling in his doodle diary – it's where he does his best imagine-ding," he said. "He draws all his thinks and ideas and dreams and everything. He started with mostly biggin bees but now he's in his diner-saurs and robots and aliens phase..."

"Already don't care," said Daisy, holding her open hand inches from Lucky's face. "So, why put a door here, bone-bag? And, more importantly, why didn't we come out of this door instead of a door all the way down in the valley? We would have found Stan-fan here ages ago."

"Ah, but *this* door is not an entrance, it is an *exit*," explained Skeleton Keys.

"An exit?" repeated Lucky. "So, it's not a door to nowhere?"

With a frustrated grunt, Daisy grabbed the handle and pushed open the door. She stomped through and emerged, disappointedly, on the other side. She let out a growl. "Looks like nowhere to me," she said.

"Ah, but you do not have this," said Skeleton Keys. He held up the third finger on his right hand and brandished it dramatically. "No one can *truly* open this door without the *Key to the Kingdom*."

"The Kingdom?" snapped Daisy. She pointed at the skeleton's finger. "You told me that was the *Key to Nothing in Particular...*"

"Ah, yes, well, I may have been slightly less than truth-filled about that," Skeleton Keys admitted a little sheepishly. "You do so revel in wreaking havoc, Daisy – if I had told you about the Kingdom, you would surely have insisted upon spoiling it."

"You've got me there," said Daisy with a shrug. "Now let me into your silly Kingdom right now or I'll—"

"Wait!" Lucky's cry rang across the hill. He was gazing in wide-eyed wonderment at Daisy. Light framed her in the open doorway.

"What are you staring at, you grapefruit?" Daisy snarled. "Anyone who stares at me gets a poke in the eye and another up the nose."

"Something's joggling in my brain..." Lucky murmured, rubbing his bruised head. With a **"Stanley!"** he suddenly bounded towards Daisy in urgent hops. Daisy raised an eyebrow before swiftly swinging the door shut. One almighty THUD later, Lucky was sprawled on the grass, rubbing his forehead.

"Daisy!" Skeleton Keys howled, helping Lucky to his feet. "Bones 'n' buckles, what were you thinking?"

"I was thinking if I closed the door, this daft mango would run head first into it," Daisy said, poking her head round the side of the door frame. "It's nice when things work out."

"My head..." groaned Lucky, and a wide grin appeared across his face. "Daisy, you bumped my brain back to where it lives!"

"Great, let's do it again," Daisy suggested.

"We shall do no such thing," insisted Skeleton Keys. "Figment, are you saying you remember what happened to Stanley?"

"The door was open..." Lucky said, his memories flooding back. "It was light outside but dark inside. Stanley was there with ... someone else."

"Someone else?" repeated Skeleton Keys.

"I ran towards him but the door swung shut," continued Lucky. "I banged my biggin head on it. By the time my brain had stopped spinning, Stanley was ... gone."

"Gone ... through? Impossible!" said Skeleton Keys. "Why, even if the door was opened from the other side, no one would have let your friend into the Kingdom, figment. It is, not to put too fine 'n' dandy a point on it, the First Rule of the Kingdom – *No Humans Allowed.*"

"But – but Stanley is humans!" cried Lucky nervously.

"*Exactly*," said Skeleton Keys. "Which makes your friend's disappearance impossibly confuddling and confuddlingly impossible."

"You're stalling, bone-bag," Daisy said. "Now open the door to the Kingdom before I make you."

"I suppose it couldn't hurt to pop in for a visit," the skeleton said to himself with a sudden air of excitement. "After all, I have not seen her in an age..."

"Her?" blurted Daisy. "Her, who?"

Skeleton Keys did not answer. Instead, he dusted off his jacket, straightened his cuffs and tugged down his waistcoat. "Fret not, figment! If your friend is in the Kingdom, I will find him!"

With that, Skeleton Keys slipped the *Key to the Kingdom* into the lock.

"Hang on, Stanley, we're coming!" Lucky called out.

"Wait, we're not taking the tangerine with us, are we?" Daisy said with a grimace and Skeleton Keys shot her a look. "Ugh, *fine*, but I'm not babysitting. So, what *is* this silly, stupid Kingdom, anyway?"

Skeleton Keys turned the key with a

CLICK
CLUNK.

"Promise to behave yourself," he said. "And I will show you."

CHAPTER FOUR

WELCOME TO THE KINGDOM

(LADY BYRD KNOWS BEST)

"Welcome to the King—" Skeleton Keys barely had time to open the door before Lucky pushed past him in a bounding hop and leaped through the door frame.

"Staaanleeey!" Lucky cried at the top of his voice. "Stanley, it's me! It's Lucky! I'm unimagine-dairy now!"

The first thing Lucky noticed was that Stanley was nowhere to be seen. As his eyes darted left and right, he realized that he was no longer on a bitter, freezing hill at the crack of dawn. Rather, he was standing on a pebble beach in the warm, skin-soothing sunshine of mid-morning. The sky above was eggshell blue and fulsome clouds hung, unmoving, in the air. A greenish ocean stretched out behind them as still as a rock pool. Beyond the beach Lucky saw another hill, but nothing like the bare and lonely ones he had left behind him. Built upon this hill's gentle, rising curve stood a large village. Among endlessly winding stone paths, steep marble steps and vibrant, manicured lawns stood numerous narrow townhouses, rising up and up to the horizon. No two were alike and each was painted in its own unique colour. Lucky saw shades of blue, red, yellow, lilac and cream he did not know existed – curious, gentle pastels that immediately calmed his nerves. Perhaps it wasn't so bad that his friend had found himself here.

All he needed to do was find him.

"This place is silly and stupid," said Daisy, following huffily behind. "Too silly nice and too stupid quiet."

"And I'd be grinnering glad if it remained that way, Daisy, so please try hard not to be yourself," Skeleton Keys said, pulling the door shut behind him. "Your only ambition should be to find this figment's—"

"Where is he?" Lucky asked, peering up and down the beach. "Where's Stanley?"

"He must have been here some time – perhaps he went for a toddle-off," Skeleton Keys suggested. "Fret not! We shall simply have to look for—"

"*Greetings!*"

The word rang out from a brass speaker secured to the door frame. The tinny voice made Lucky all but jump out of his fur.

"*Welcome to the Kingdom,*" the message

continued. *"We are so happy you have decided to join us. Please make yourself at home, by making yourself a home! Here's to your new life, filled with good imaginings and endless possibilities,"* the announcement continued. *"And remember, Lady Byrd knows best!"*

"Lady Byrd knows best!" repeated Skeleton Keys with giddy enthusiasm.

"Ladybird?" said Daisy with a sneer. "Who's Ladybird?"

"Lady Byrd is ... fantabulant," Skeleton Keys said, his milk-white eyes glazing over as he stared wistfully into the middle distance. "Milady and I—"

"'Milady'? Pfff, what is she, a silly princess?" Daisy interrupted.

"I shall have you know, Milady is

the reason this fantabulant place exists at all," Skeleton Keys declared, and began striding up the beach. "Follow me! If anyone knows where your friend is, figment, it is Milady..."

"We don't need help – we can find Stanfan's friend on our own," huffed Daisy, trying to keep up with the skeleton as Lucky hopped eagerly past her.

"Ah, but Lady Byrd knows best!" the skeleton said. In moments he'd cleared the beach and slipped down a narrow alleyway between two pale blue houses. "Though she will not be gladdened to learn of Stanley Strange's presence here. The truth of the fact is, no human has ever set foot in the Kingdom ... until today."

"Who *does* live in this dump then?" Daisy asked as she and Lucky pursued the skeleton down the alleyway. Skeleton Keys stood aside to reveal a wide piazza surrounded by tall, colourful buildings.

"Why, they do," the skeleton replied. "With luck, Stanley Strange should stick out like a sore thumb-bone..."

As Lucky peered out from the alleyway, he was confronted with a sight that made his jaw drop and his nose twitch. The piazza was bustling with villagers, each one more weird and wonderful than the last: a teddy bear with a head as wide as a small car ... a garden gnome with an old telephone for a hat ... a huge, rolling ball of fur with a blue bow in its hair ... a hedgehog with a unicorn's horn riding a rainbow ... bizarre creatures of every description.

"Who are they?" Lucky whispered.

"Unimaginaries, obviously," said Daisy. "But what are they all doing here?"

"This is their home," replied Skeleton Keys. "And it was Ol' Mr Keys who brought them here."

CHAPTER FIVE

THE SEARCH BEGINS

(LUCKY MEETS THE LOCALS)

"An hour ago it seemed absurd
That I could be besotted
But now I have met my Lady Byrd
My heart is fair garroted!"
—SK

"I don't see Stanley..." said Lucky as they made their way through the piazza among the crowd of unimaginaries. "Where's Stanley?"

"Ugh, change the record, you tangerine – we'll find your friend satsuma or later," grunted Daisy.

"Mr Keys!" said a giant banana with two faces as it wandered by. "It's been a while! You must pop by my new pottery shop – I couldn't have imagined opening it without you."

"If there is time, Banana with Two Faces!"

replied the skeleton with a wave. "Grinnering to see you have settled in!"

As Skeleton Keys continued to greet one strangely contented unimaginary after another, Daisy eyed everything and everyone with suspicion.

"So, why did you bring them all here, bone-bag? Is this place some kind of evil unimaginary dumping ground, or did they just want to get away from you?"

"I will have you know, the Kingdom is a haven, Daisy," Skeleton Keys replied. "A sort of retirement home for unimaginary friends."

"Retirement?" repeated Daisy suspiciously. "Being unimaginary's not a job – if it was I wouldn't do it."

"True. But unimaginaries do not age – they remain exactly as they are in the moment they are unimagined," explained Skeleton Keys. "In time, those who have imagined them inevitably grow old and pass away. An unimaginary might be left all alone, without the friend who unimagined them in the first place. The Kingdom is a place where unimaginaries may go to live out their existence."

"So, they're stuck here?" asked Daisy, rather enjoying the possibility. "Like in prison?"

"Prison? Crumcrinkles, no!" replied the skeleton in horror. He gestured back to the door on the beach, still visible between two colourful buildings. "The exit is not locked – unimaginaries may leave at any time. But no one ever has. In one hundred years, no one but Ol' Mr Keys has opened that door."

"Except for whoever let Stan-fan's friend in," Daisy corrected him.

"Indeed – I can only think someone let Stanley in by *accident*," mused Skeleton Keys. "No doubt Milady will be able to help us find your friend, figment! Stick with me and you shall surely be reunited with— Figment?"

But Lucky had already disappeared into the crowd of unimaginaries, hopping all the way to the other side of the square in search of his friend. With no sign of Stanley, he leaped in front of a burly greenish troll with large tusks and huge, hairy arms.

"Excuse me, have you seen Stanley?" Lucky asked. "He's my biggin best friend in all the world and he came through the Door to Nowhere, which isn't a door to nowhere, it's actually a door to here."

"I haven't the faintest whiff of what you're on about, fella," said the troll. "Are you new here?"

"I'm new everywhere – I'm only just unimagine-dairy," explained Lucky. He made circles with his fingers and thumbs and held them over his eyes. "Stanley's got glasses for reading and doodling and seeing stuff – have you seen him?"

"Glasses, eh?" said the troll. In an instant, a pair of glasses appeared out of thin air on the end of the monster's nose. "Like this?"

"No biggin *way*," said Lucky with a gasp, as other unimaginaries began to gather round.

"New glasses, Trolliver?" asked a turtle in a brightly coloured sweater.

"This fella's lost his friend, Turtleneck,"
explained Trolliver. "I'm trying to sniff out if
I've seen him."

"Have *you* seen Stanley?" Lucky asked the
turtle. "He's got twenty-eight teeth and a
stripy hat."

"Like this?" said the turtle, a striped baseball
cap suddenly appeared on the top of her head.

"Or more like this?" suggested a creature
made up of seven different types of root
vegetable. A moment later, a cowboy hat
materialized atop the parsnip he called a head.

"I mean, not really," admitted Lucky. "But
how are you doing that?"

"Imagining, naturally," replied Veginald.
"In the Kingdom, anything you imagine can
be—"

"There you are!" came a cry. Lucky turned
to see Skeleton Keys and Daisy break through
the crowd. "I would be gladdened if you did

not go running off like that, figment," the skeleton added. "We do not want to lose you too now, do we?"

"I have no problem with it," Daisy noted.

"Nobody's even seen him," Lucky said with a sad sniff. "How come nobody's seen Stanley?"

"I cannot imagine," the skeleton confessed. He pointed to the very top of the hill, where stood an especially tall house, painted in a striking bright green. "But if anyone can find him, it is Lady Byrd."

CHAPTER SIX

LADY BYRD

(THE ATRIUM)

"Lady Byrd, how do I love thee?
Let me count the ways
I love you to my very bones
You leave me in a daze!"
—SK

As Lucky followed Skeleton Keys and Daisy up winding streets and narrow lanes towards Lady Byrd's house, he made sure to ask everyone he saw whether they had seen his best friend.

"Have you seen Stanley?" he asked a cat dressed as a clown. "He's got a birthmark on his left knee and he's allergic to tomatoes."

But Catilla the Fun had not seen Stanley.

"Have you seen Stanley?" he asked a girl swimming about in a floating soup bowl. "He only likes red apples and he can do a

59

handstand against a wall..."

But Alpha Beth Soup had not seen Stanley.

"You'd remember Stanley," he assured a boy with a clock for a head, thrusting Stanley's sketchbook under his nose. "He drew this picture of a diner-saur. Have you seen him?"

But Tick-Tock Tim-Tom just shrugged.

In fact, no one had seen him. As Lucky returned Stanley's sketchbook to his pouch, he was left with nothing but questions. Who had opened the door? How had no one even seen his friend? And of course one question rang around his head like a bell: where was Stanley?

By the time they reached the green house, Lucky felt his heart sinking deeper in his chest.

"Do you really think Milady Byrd can help me find Stanley, Mr Keys?" he asked, staring up at the house. It was the tallest building in the Kingdom, with an impressive domed roof made from a rainbow of coloured glass.

"Lady Byrd knows best," the skeleton replied. As they approached the door – a perfect circle of polished wood – Skeleton Keys adjusted his cravat. "How do I look?" he asked.

"Like a walking nightmare, obviously," said Daisy, narrowing her eyes. "Wait, are you trying to *impress* this lady-bug, bone-bag?"

"Of course not! Ol' Mr Keys has always been pridesome of his appearance," replied the skeleton, trying to inspect his reflection in his polished shoes. With a long sigh, he added, "Anyway, Milady's life has always been here in the Kingdom, while mine has been out there, in the real world and beyond…"

With that, he rapped once on the door. A pause sat heavily in the air.

Daisy tutted. She'd never seen the skeleton wait for a door to be opened – he usually just let himself in. She was already reaching for the door as it suddenly swung open, all by itself.

"No biggin way," Lucky whispered in awe, and followed Skeleton Keys and Daisy inside. He found himself in a grand atrium, which stretched all the way to the top of the house. The floor was a soft carpet of grass and moss and flowers, and plants of every description grew from the walls. In the centre of the atrium, an ancient, knotted tree reached up and up, creating a canopy of leaves below the skylight of coloured glass.

"Smells like wet garden in here," Daisy grumbled, reaching behind her head to pinch her nose.

Lucky gazed up to the top of the tree. *It would take all biggin day to climb it,* he thought. A moment later, he heard a low, soft buzzing sound and saw a bee fly lazily past his face. The bee circled him once, then twice. As it started a third orbit of his head, Lucky turned to look at it.

Suddenly, it wasn't there any more.

"What...?" whispered Lucky.

"Lady Byrd?" called Skeleton Keys in an enthusiastic whisper. "Milady, are you—"

"Mr Keys! As I live and breathe!" came a cry. As Skeleton Keys glanced up, his jaw fell open – in fact, it fell off entirely, landing on the grass with a

FLUD.

Daisy rolled her eyes.

Lucky looked up to see a figure descend from high above, fluttering down from the leafy canopy on diaphanous wings that beat so quickly they were a blur. She was a curious sight, as much an insect as she was a human being. Despite more or less human proportions, her arms and legs were spindly and segmented, with hands and feet like hooked claws. Her eyes were large black orbs and long antennae grew from her head. Two curved red 'shells' spread out behind her but, the moment she landed, they folded around her to form a wide, cone-like dress.

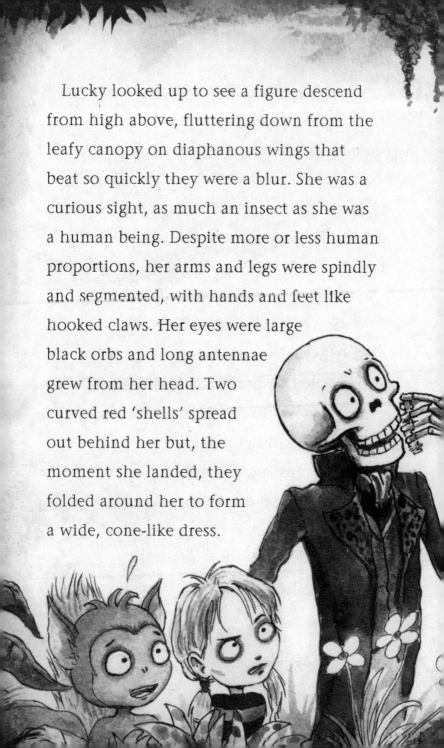

"Excuse me," began Lucky. "Have you seen my fr—"

"Miayygee!" Skeleton Keys said again, urgently replacing his jaw. Then he bowed so low that his skull rubbed along the grassy floor. "How fine 'n' fantabulantly fabulush to behold your majestic milady-ness!"

"What a surprise, Mr Keys," said Lady Byrd, her voice a soft coo. "I am afraid you caught me ... napping in my tree. The business of running a Kingdom takes its toll."

"A dozen – no, a *hundred* humbling apologies, Milady," said Skeleton Keys, his voice breathless with admiration. "Had I known, I would not have dreamed of waking you in a thousand – no, a million years!"

"Excuse me, I'm looking for my—" Lucky started.

"Who are your friends, Mr Keys?" Lady Byrd asked, peering down at Lucky and Daisy. "New additions to the Kingdom, I presume?"

"Live here? No chance," Daisy scoffed. "I'm Daisy, and I'm too much trouble for this silly place, *Bugatha*."

"Daisy!" snapped Skeleton Keys.

"We're used to troublemakers in the Kingdom, Daisy," said Lady Byrd with a smile.

"We have ways of keeping the peace and quiet."

"Yet more apologies, Milady," Skeleton Keys said with another bow. "My partner-in-problem-solving is flabbergastingly lacking in manners."

"I'm looking for my—" Lucky began.

"Partner? Daisy, you lucky thing," Lady Byrd cooed. "What an honour, to be partnered with such a supremely skilful skeleton."

"Pfff, you must have your antennae crossed, Bugatha," Daisy sneered. "Bone-bag's only skill is how much he annoys me."

"Did he not tell you?" Lady Byrd chuckled. "How characteristically humble..."

"Tell me what?" Daisy snapped.

"Why, without Mr Keys, there would be no Kingdom at all," Lady Byrd answered. "He created it."

"Milady is too, too kind," Skeleton Keys said, bowing again. "Too, too, too—"

"When Mr Keys and I first met, I had only been unimagined for a few moments," Lady Byrd interrupted. "But I already knew that I could not bear to live in the real world – the *human* world. Mr Keys vowed to build me a new home. He took me to a world he called the Nothing in Particular. I was content among the nothingness, but Mr Keys had other ideas – he took his imagination from inside his head and planted it at the very heart of the Nothing in Particular. Through the power of Mr Keys' wild imagination, I was able to create this Kingdom."

"*Your* Kingdom, Milady," Skeleton Keys said.

"Wait, you gave up your imagination for Bugatha?" Daisy growled. "You soppy skeleton! That's why there's never a decent idea in your silly, stupid—"

"STANLEY!"

The word rang out and echoed through

the atrium. Everyone turned to see Lucky, his face flushed a dark blue and his fists clenched.

"I'm looking for Stanley Strange!" Lucky howled. "He's my biggin best friend in the world and – and I lost him!"

"...Lost him?" repeated Lady Byrd.

"He's all I've got ... all I've ever had," Lucky said, tears in his eyes. "Stanley unimagine-did me."

Lady Byrd clasped a hand over her mouth in horror.

"Unimagined you?" Her voice was a shivering whisper. "You mean, he's your – he's *human*?"

"He's human and he's *here*," said Daisy with a lopsided grin. "Looks like somebody broke your rule, Bugatha."

"Mr Keys, is this true?" she said, not taking her eyes off Lucky. "Is there a human in the Kingdom?"

"'Twas not my doing, Milady!" insisted Skeleton Keys. "But it does seem so – the figment is convinced that his friend travelled through the Exit door to the Kingdom. It appears someone let him in."

"Let him in...?" repeated Lady Byrd. "Then, where in the Kingdom is he?"

"That is rather the confuddling bit," admitted Skeleton Keys. "We have searched high and low – not to mention far and wide – but have seen neither hide nor hair of the ankle-sprout."

"Please can you help me find him, Milady Byrd?" Lucky pleaded, wiping a tear from his cheek.

Lady Byrd leaned down towards Lucky, her insect eyes inspecting him closely.

"Lucky, is it?" she said softly. "Tell me, Lucky, does your friend have round glasses and a striped hat?"

"A striped— Yes!" Lucky cried. "How'd you know that? Have you seen him?"

Lady Byrd held out her hand, and a small, round mirror materialized in an instant, its handle clasped between her spindly fingers. As Lucky held his breath in amazement, Lady Byrd held the mirror up to his face. He'd never seen his reflection before, but he barely noticed his orange fur or blue monkey-like face. Lucky noticed something else entirely.

He was suddenly wearing a pair of glasses and a striped hat.

CHAPTER SEVEN

GOOD IMAGININGS ONLY

(THE KINGDOM'S POWER)

*"The course of wild imagining
never did run smooth."*
—SK

"How'd you biggin do that?" asked
Lucky, pulling off the hat and glasses
and staring at them in awe.

"It was not me, Lucky – it was *you*,"
explained Lady Byrd, the mirror in her hand
evaporating. "You were thinking about your
friend and his glasses and hat just appeared
on your head. You must have imagined them
without knowing it."

"I imagine-did?" said Lucky. He looked
down at his hands to see the glasses and hat
suddenly vanish before his eyes. Lady Byrd

glided across the room and out of the open doorway into the street.

"Everything you see before you – the whole Kingdom – is imagined," Lady Byrd explained as everyone followed her outside. "But that is only part of the Kingdom's power."

"Ugh, what *else* have you been keeping to yourself, bone-bag?" said Daisy. Lady Byrd turned to her and held out a spindly hand in front of her face. In an instant, a flowerpot appeared from nowhere in Lady Byrd's palm. A moment later, a green stem extended from the soil, growing from a bud to a bright red rose before her very eyes.

"I hate magic tricks," tutted Daisy.

"No tricks ... imagining." Lady Byrd smiled. "Here in the Kingdom, anything you imagine can become *real* in an instant. Your imaginings will remain real for as long as you wish," she continued, pointing up at the atrium. "I imagined the atrium a hundred years ago and it has stood ever since. But this flower…" She blew lightly upon the rose, and both flower and pot vanished as if they were never there.

"No biggin way," said Lucky, making pairs of glasses and striped beanie hats appear, one after the other, until a pile lay at his feet. "Look, Mr Keys, I'm imagine-ding!"

"Why didn't anybody tell me about this when we got here?" Daisy grunted, terrible thoughts already flooding her mind. She held out her arms, palms up, as if waiting for a gift, and closed her eyes. "*Fireworks*," she said. "I imagine enough fireworks to give every last one of these soggy bog rolls a proper scare."

There was a pause. Daisy opened both eyes and stared at her empty hands.

"Daisy—" began Skeleton Keys.

"Shut up, you fibbing bag of bones," she said. She folded her arms and glowered at Lady Byrd. "Where's my fireworks, Bugatha? Your Kingdom is as broken as your silly rule."

"As I told you, Daisy, we have ways of keeping the peace and quiet," explained Lady Byrd with a smile. "The Second Rule of the Kingdom: *Good Imaginings Only*. Bad imaginings cannot be made real."

"Good imaginings? What's that supposed to mean?" asked Daisy. "Fireworks are good – especially when I hide them under bone-bag's chair."

"It is a matter of intent – when it comes to imagining, the Kingdom does not allow for *unkindness*," said Lady Byrd. "It may be a hard concept for you to grasp."

"You don't get to decide what's good and what's not," Daisy grunted.

"Daisy, please be a little less *you* for the moment," Skeleton Keys implored her. "We must focus on the matter in—"

"Shut it, bone-bag, I'm imagining." Daisy squeezed her eyes shut again. "*Dog* ... I imagine an angry, bitey, bad-breath dog to chase you all around this stupid village and back again. I imagine it!"

But despite Daisy's wildest attempts at imagining, a dog did not appear.

Lucky, meanwhile, gazed down the street. A pair of passing unimaginaries, one a snowman, the other a pink cow, imagined brightly coloured bluebirds as they walked, which appeared and disappeared above the unimaginaries' heads.

As Daisy growled, trying in vain to conjure one terrible imagining after another, Lucky had an idea. He closed his eyes and whispered so quietly that he could barely hear his own voice.

"Stanley," he said. "I imagine Stanley."

CHAPTER EIGHT

BYRD SONG

(WISHFUL THINKING)

"O, Lady Byrd! A finer IF
You could not ask to meet
But with the merest whistle
She could sing you straight to sleep!"
—SK

Lucky was sure he had never imagined anything so wildly as he imagined Stanley Strange. He saw him in his mind's eye, in his big coat and his glasses and his beanie hat. When he was sure he had imagined his best friend as well as anyone had ever imagined anything, he opened his eyes.

But Stanley was nowhere to be seen. There was just the Kingdom, stretching out below them – and a girl with a backwards head.

"Angry wasps ... stink bombs ... a tank!" Daisy growled, eyes closed and fists clenched.

At last, she opened her eyes. "This silly Kingdom is *stupid*," she snarled, glowering at Lady Byrd and jabbing her finger. "I don't need imaginings to make trouble! I'm Daisy – I've got a backwards head and a bad attitude. I'm more trouble in my *sleep* than you could possibly imagine, Bugatha."

"Daisy...!" Skeleton Keys snapped. A smile flashed across Daisy's face as, for the first time, she saw Lady Byrd bristle.

"Yes, that will do, young lady," Lady Byrd said. "On the grand scale of rudeness, pointing is second only to whistling."

"Well, unless there's a pointing rule, you can't stop me, now can you?" Daisy sneered, her outstretched finger hovering near Lady Byrd's left nostril.

"True – just as you cannot stop me whistling," said Lady Byrd. With that, she put her lips together and let out a sound not quite like any other. Daisy didn't just hear it – she *felt* it – a strange, lulling hum that travelled from her ears to her toes in an instant. Before she knew what was happening, her eyelids grew heavy and her head began to loll forwards against her back. A moment later, she was asleep where she stood. Lady Byrd imagined a bright green beanbag beneath Daisy's feet before she slumped on to it and began snoring contentedly.

"No biggin way," Lucky said under his breath.

"Crumcrinkles, I probably should have warned her about your *Byrd Song*," said Skeleton Keys with a shake of his head.

"Just a little ditty – a longer song could have sent her to sleep for a year," Lady Byrd explained. "As it is, Daisy should be awake and back to her unpleasant self in a few hours."

"Milady knows best..." Skeleton Keys replied. In an instant of imagining, Lady Byrd conjured a bright green pram in front of him. He scooped Daisy up from the beanbag and placed her in the pram. "To be frankly, Ol' Mr Keys could do with a little peace and quiet."

"Then all that's left is to deal with our ... human problem," said Lady Byrd. She turned to Lucky, to find him wiping tears from his eyes.

"I couldn't imagine him," he said with a sniff. "Why couldn't I imagine Stanley? It was a good imagine-ding, wasn't it?"

Lady Byrd kneeled down in front of Lucky.

"Did you imagine?" she asked. "Or did you wish?"

"I-I'm not sure," Lucky admitted, wiping more tears away. "What's the difference?"

"I lost a friend too, once," said Lady Byrd, her voice cracking a little. "When I first came to the Kingdom, I tried to imagine him, but I could not bring him back. In time, I realized that I wasn't imagining, I was *wishing* for his return. I wanted him to be real. But *nothing* in the Kingdom is truly real. We are figments of imagining in an imagined world."

"I don't know what that means," Lucky admitted.

Lady Byrd lowered her head with a strange, shivering sigh. "It means I will help you," she said at last. "Fortunately – I have an ace up my sleeve."

"But you don't have sleeves," Lucky said.

Lady Byrd smiled. She conjured a small, brass bell from the air and gave it a little shake. It made no sound. "There," she added. "He'll be with you in a moment."

"He? He, who?" Skeleton Keys repeated in confusion.

With a sudden

BWOOOF!

– an explosion of bright red smoke filled the air. Skeleton Keys stumbled blindly backwards, coughing and spluttering. Then, as the smoke began to clear, he saw a tall, broad figure, half hidden in the haze of scarlet fog.

"Hello, funny fingers!" the figure boomed.

"Crumcrinkles! Not him ... anyone but *him*," Skeleton Keys whispered in horror. "Anyone but *ImagiNathan*."

CHAPTER NINE

IMAGINATHAN

(NOTHING BUT TROUBLE)

From *Ol' Mr Keys Unimaginable Adventures,*
No. 866 – Menace of the Magenta Magician

Appearing in a puff of smoke
With plots above his station
Has e'er there been a single IF
As maddening as Nathan?

As the smoke began to clear, Lucky got a good look at the figure who had, it seemed, appeared in the street from nowhere. He was tall, broad-shouldered, and dressed in a bright red tuxedo and top hat. In fact, everything about him was red, from skin to eyes to teeth to the curled moustache that seemed to extend out forever from his top lip.

"Mr Keys, you remember ImagiNathan," said Lady Byrd, as Skeleton Keys placed his skull in his hands. "I believe you dropped him off on your last visit."

"Funny fingers, you son of a dog bone!" cried ImagiNathan, twirling a red wand around his fingers. "How in the name of my awesome imaginings are you? Still sticking your keys into other people's business?"

"Cheese 'n' biscuits..." Skeleton Keys groaned through gritted teeth. "How are you settling in, Nathan?"

"It's *ImagiNathan*, and you know it," ImagiNathan replied with a hint of sharpness. "The Scarlet Sorcerer! The Crimson Conjuror! The Magenta Magician!" He glanced at Daisy, slumbering in her pram, and raised a red eyebrow. "Didn't take you as a family man, funny fingers," he added.

"Daisy is my partner-in-problem—"

"I have a job for you, ImagiNathan," Lady Byrd interrupted.

"I'm ImagiNathan – I can do anything I put my mind to," ImagiNathan declared, and a polished green apple suddenly appeared in his hand.

"I don't doubt it," Lady Byrd said with a smile. "Which is why I would like you to find this unimaginary's friend."

"*What?*" Skeleton Keys howled. "Milady, not *Nathan*...!"

"Looking for a friend, are you?" said ImagiNathan, leaning in to inspect Lucky as he chomped on his apple. "Not a problem – you stick with ImagiNathan and friends will be flocking around you just to get to *me*."

"I've got a friend but I lost him," said Lucky, wiping chunks of apple from his face. "His name is—"

"Good for you!" boomed ImagiNathan. He turned to Lady Byrd as a bouquet of roses appeared in his hand. With a wink he added, "Did you really bring me here just to meet this little cantaloupe, Lady B?"

"Not quite," admitted Lady Byrd. "It appears someone has let a *human* into the Kingdom."

"A human? Naughty, naughty!" tutted ImagiNathan. "Left the Exit door open, did you, funny fingers?"

"I did no such thing!" Skeleton Keys said. "I will have you know—"

"Mr Keys tried his best but he cannot find the human," continued Lady Byrd. "I thought if anyone could track him down, it would surely be ImagiNathan, my absolute *favourite* miracle worker..."

"Is it true? Can you biggin really find Stanley?" Lucky asked ImagiNathan, hopping up and down on the spot.

"I'm ImagiNathan," replied the magician, conjuring a blue balloon out of thin air and immediately popping it with an imagined pin. "I can do anything I put my mind to."

"Milady, a word!" Skeleton Keys hissed. In two long strides he sidled up to Lady Byrd, almost treading on Lucky. "Forgive me, Milady," he added in an urgent whisper, "but are you sure about this? Nathan is—"

"*ImagiNathan*," said Lucky, trying to be helpful.

"...Is nothing but trouble!" continued Skeleton Keys. "By my bones, he is one of the most flabbergastingly frustrating, do-no-good unimaginaries I have ever had the misfortune to meet! Betwixt his ability to create illusions and desperate desire to cause maddening mischief, he had Ol' Mr Keys at my wits' end. Why, it was only my promise of a place where his illusions could be made real that put an end to his misfortunate misbehaviour!"

"And ImagiNathan has made a happy home for himself here, and been little or no trouble to anyone," Lady Byrd assured him. "Since the Kingdom allows him only to create good imaginings, I am sure he is ready to prove himself more than useful."

"Useful? He is a scallywaggling mischief-maker!" Skeleton Keys protested. "Why, I would not be surprised if it was he who let Stanley Strange into the Kingdom..."

"Jealous, funny fingers?" grinned ImagiNathan, slapping Skeleton Keys on the back so hard he stumbled into Lucky again. "Don't worry, you put your slippers on and give those old bones a rest. I'll be back in the wave of a wand..."

Another BLOOOF! of blinding red smoke filled the air. By the time it had cleared, ImagiNathan had disappeared.

"You see?" said Lady Byrd. "ImagiNathan is on the case – no doubt he will reunite you with Stanley Strange soon enough."

"Thank you, Milady Byrd," said Lucky, happier tears now welling in his eyes.

Lady Byrd leaned closer. "I am sure your friend is fine," she whispered. "And wherever he is, I am sure he is dreaming of you."

"Dreaming?" repeated Lucky.

"Thinking," Lady Byrd said quickly. "Thinking of you."

With that, she turned back towards her atrium and swept through the doorway. "All will be well! Lady Byrd knows best!" she added, before the door slammed shut.

"Lady Byrd knows best..." muttered Skeleton Keys, sounding wholly less convinced than before. With a sigh, he grabbed the Daisy-filled pram and started pushing it at speed back down the hill.

"How long do you think it'll take Mr ImagiNathan to find Stanley, Mr Keys?" asked Lucky, hopping excitedly after him. "One minute? Two? I bet one!"

"Nathan is not going to find your friend," insisted the skeleton.

"He – he isn't?" Lucky said nervously.

"No, we are," said Skeleton Keys with grim determination.

"We are going to find Stanley Strange before that foulsome flabbergaster, figment. The race is on!"

M e again, dallywanglers! Forgive my intruding like a frog with a foghorn, just as things are hotting up, but I wanted to be certain you were suitably entertained by the tale I chose to call *The Wild Imaginings of Stanley Strange*. Where can that boy be? And – dogs 'n' cats! – why would Lady Byrd send that rottering rugslugger Nathan to find him? Will all end well and gladdening or are events about to take a terrible turn for the troublesome? I cannot imagine!

And speaking of which, please do not feel sorry for Ol' Mr Keys just because I am no longer possessed of a wild imagination! Surrendering it to create the Kingdom was the very least I could do for Lady Byrd. Milady's tale is one of love and woe, and a secret only she and Ol' Mr Keys know.

Longish ago, when Ol' Mr Keys was barely a

century old, there was a child, who had spent much of his short life languishing in his sick bed. While he lay awake, wondering if he would ever be well, he imagined a friend by the name of Lady Byrd, whose soft and gentle song helped to lull him to restful, painless sleep. And though their friendship salved the boy's soul, his body would not recover. Perhaps the boy knew he was dying ... perhaps that is why he imagined his friend so wildly and so well that, all of a suddenly, Lady Byrd became real. Perhaps he thought her song would help to soothe his passing ... or perhaps he just did not want to be alone. Either way, in her first moments as an unimaginary friend, Lady Byrd sang the boy to sleep for the last time.

With the boy gone, Milady's grief consumed her. By the time I found her, she had already decided that she could not bear to look – not even take the slightest gaddly gander! – upon another human face. She begged me to help her escape the real world. As it so happened, my *Key to Nothing in Particular* led to a world of nothing in particular, so I decided I would build her a home there – a place where Milady could have anything she imagined.

Cheese 'n' biscuits, such a place could only exist with the limitless power of imagination at its disposal! So it was that I plucked my own imagination from my skull – a fiddly feat, even for this fantabulant bag o' bones! – and planted it at the very heart of the Nothing in Particular. In an instant, the Nothing in Particular was transformed into a world where anything a mind could imagine can become real. My *Key to Nothing in Particular* became the *Key to the Kingdom.*

"Your Kingdom," Lady Byrd told me. But, in truth, it was always *hers.* She vowed never to leave. At last she seemed heart-warmed and happy, and so Ol' Mr Keys was happy too.

Soon, other unimaginaries whose friends had long since passed also began to look for a way to escape the real world. Milady welcomed them with open arms. I continued to transport adrift unimaginaries to a new home. Thus and therefore, the Kingdom began to grow.

To keep the peace and quiet of her new life, Lady Byrd suggested two rules – *No Humans Allowed* and a single limitation to the Kingdom's endless possibilities or, as Milady put it, *Good Imaginings Only*.

I have often wondered whether Milady misses the real world. But she assures me that in a hundred years, she has never so much as peeked outside the Kingdom.

Crumcrinkles, the Kingdom! We must return there forthwith and continue our adventure! Lucky's best friend is still missing, Daisy has been forced into forty winks by Lady Byrd, and – would you believe it! – that rottering rugslugger Nathan thinks he can find Stanley Strange before me! Who does he think he is? I cannot imagine! But I do know this:

Strange things can happen when *Strange* imaginations run wild...

CHAPTER TEN

THE DINOSAUR

(RACE TO FIND STANLEY)

Lucky hopped after Skeleton Keys down the winding lanes of the Kingdom as fast as his tiny orange legs could carry him.

"I don't understand," he puffed, trying to keep up as the skeleton pushed the pram (with the still-slumbering Daisy inside) down street after lane. "I thought Mr ImagiNathan was finding Stanley..."

"Puffwinkles! *Nathan* could not find a needle in a needle-stack – he has less chance of finding Stanley Strange than I have of possessing fingernails," said Skeleton Keys,

ducking down another street. "How he has hoodwinkled Milady into imagining he is anything but a scammering do-no-good, I cannot imagine! And while we are on the subject, so *what* if I cannot imagine? Does it make him better than me?"

"Uhh—" was all a baffled Lucky could muster.

"Exactly!" said Skeleton Keys. "No, it is Ol' Mr Keys who will find your friend, figment. The clock is ticking – keep your eye sockets peeled for any sign of Stanley strangeness!"

Lucky picked up the pace, desperate to keep up with the manic, pram-pushing skeleton.

"Stanley!" cried Lucky, his voice echoing down the hill.

"Stanley Strange!" hollered Skeleton Keys.

"Sta—"

Lucky froze. At the end of the street a

large, dark shape was silhouetted against the Kingdom's hazy afternoon light. Lucky squinted. With all the fantastically formed unimaginaries in the Kingdom, he had no idea who or what it could be. Then the shape reared up to its full height. It bared its teeth and swished its tail, and let out a rasping growl, hot breath puffing from its nostrils.

"*Diner-saur*," whispered Lucky as the beast roared. "It's a diner-saur!"

Lucky immediately had mixed feelings. Stanley loved dinosaurs, so he was happy to be reminded of his best friend. On the other hand, the snarling, sharp-toothed monster that was currently pacing towards them seemed anything but friendly.

"Fret not! I know an *imagining* when I see one – that be-scaled beast is no more dangerous than the hat you conjured yourself," chuckled Skeleton Keys. "Remember,

all imaginings in the Kingdom must be *good*,
or they cannot be imagined at—"

The dinosaur roared. The ear-splitting cry
echoed down the street and made Lucky's
tail hair stand on end. The monster opened
its jaws and clamped them fiercely on
to a nearby bench. A moment later,
it wrenched the bench from
the ground, sending
shattered cobbles
flying. The bench
hung in the
dinosaur's
mouth
for a
moment
– then
it flung it
through
the air.

"Dogs 'n' cats!" shrieked Skeleton Keys, ducking as the bench whizzed over his head. It missed him by a hair and shattered on the ground behind him.

"It don't look biggin good to me!" squealed Lucky. The dinosaur suddenly charged, teeth bared and eyes glowing red. Skeleton Keys grabbed the sleeping Daisy out of the pram and thrust one of his key-tipped fingers, impossibly, into the wall. "This calls for the *Key to a Quick Getaway*!" he cried, turning the key with a CLICK CLUNK. In an instant, a door materialized in the wall. The skeleton pulled it open and, with a swift kick of his polished shoe, booted Lucky through the doorway.

"Uff!" Lucky wheezed as he tumbled through thin air. Though he was too terrified to realize what had happened, the *Key to a Quick Getaway* had transported him to a point high above the street. He fell, landing with a THUD upon a slanted roof of one of the Kingdom's many townhouses. A split second later, Skeleton Keys appeared from the same point in the sky, Daisy gripped under his arm.

"Dogs 'n' cats, figment, hang on to something!" The skeleton let out a shriek as he and Lucky found themselves sliding helplessly towards the roof's edge. As he skidded and tumbled, Lucky spotted the dinosaur materialize in the air and plummet on to the tiles.

"M-Mr Keys!" Lucky shrieked as the dinosaur set its sights upon him. "Diner-saur followed us!"

"At this exacting moment in time, figment," said Skeleton Keys, desperately trying to slow his descent, "that is our second most worrisome worry!"

A moment later, they both slid off the edge of the roof.

"Figment!" the skeleton shrieked, grabbing Lucky in his spare hand and, by some miracle of contortion, sinking his teeth into the roof's gutter. With Lucky in one hand and Daisy in the other, Skeleton Keys desperately clenched his jaw, the gutter creaking and cracking under the strain. With little to no idea what to do next, he glanced up. The dinosaur glowered down at him over the edge of the roof.

"Cknklnklsss...!" the skeleton uttered. As the dinosaur roared madly in his face, Skeleton Keys wished he could close his eyes...

PLOIP!

The dinosaur was suddenly enveloped in a huge, soapy bubble, which carried it into the air. The creature floated upwards, thrashing madly, but neither tooth nor claw could pierce the elastic sphere.

"Whht...?" grunted Skeleton Keys before, out of nowhere, a vivid flash of red and green feathers darted by his skull. Then another flash, this time a feathery flurry of blue and yellow. In moments, a whole flock of large, brightly coloured parrots was swooping around him. In his alarm, the skeleton's teeth slipped from the gutter but, before he could fall, the parrots grabbed him in their talons, taking hold of arms, legs, collars and tailcoats. As he held Lucky and Daisy tightly, Skeleton Keys felt the parrots lower him slowly to the ground, their many wings beating in unison.

"Crumcrinkles..." the skeleton muttered, placing Lucky on terra firma as he cradled the dozing Daisy. A second later, the parrots vanished into nothingness.

"Birds ... biggin birds saved us!" Lucky squealed, squinting through hazy light up at the roof. "W-what happened?"

The answer to Lucky's question came in the form of a BLOOOF! of red smoke. A moment later, ImagiNathan emerged from the haze, dragging the weightless, dinosaur-filled bubble behind him like a balloon on a string. He gave Lucky a wink.

"Somebody order a balloon animal?"

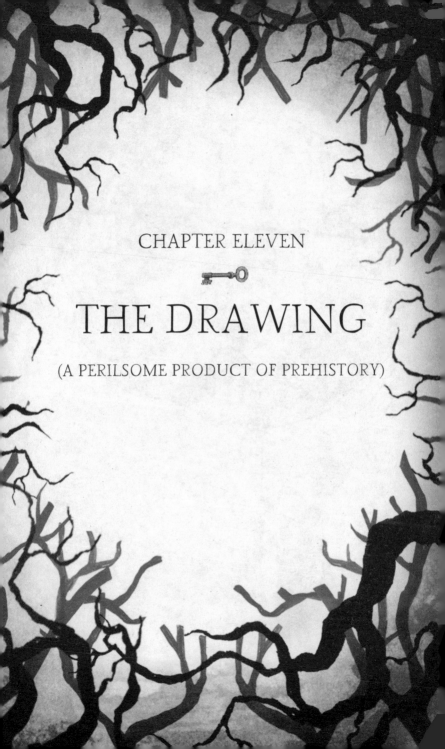

CHAPTER ELEVEN

THE DRAWING

(A PERILSOME PRODUCT OF PREHISTORY)

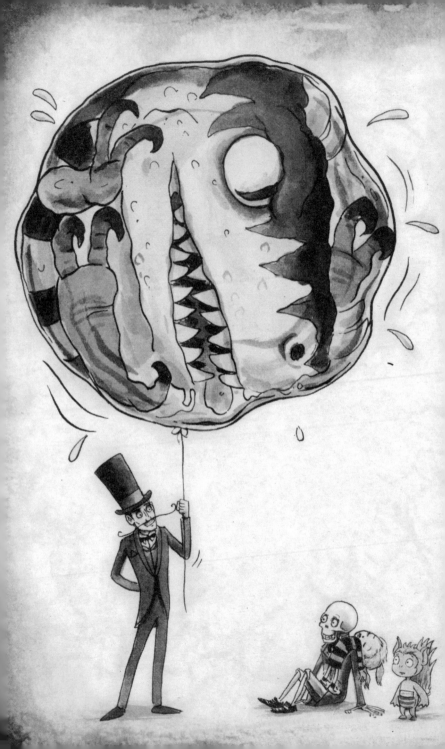

"I have never met an ImagiNathan
I didn't dislike."
—SK

"Nathan, you crunch-foot rumbleshover!" Skeleton Keys cried, shifting the sleeping Daisy from one shoulder to the other. "Your imagining nearly killed us!"

"It's *Imagi*Nathan – and what are you blithering about, funny fingers?" scoffed ImagiNathan, twirling his scarlet moustache. "Were you not just rescued by my flock of plucky parrots? My imaginings *saved* you."

"You did all that?" gasped Lucky. "You imagine-did up all those birds?"

"Birds shmirds!" Skeleton Keys howled. "Admit it, Nathan, 'twas you imagined that perilsome product of prehistory! You *live* for this sort of huff 'n' hubbub!"

"*Moi?* But I've turned over a new leaf!" ImagiNathan replied, feigning dismay at the accusation. He prodded the dinosaur-filled bubble with a scarlet finger. "Anyway, why would I imagine this beast just to snare it in my *thought bubble?*"

"You imagine-did that too?" cried an awestruck Lucky.

"No one imagines like ImagiNathan!" declared ImagiNathan. "Not like poor funny fingers here – he's been lacking in the imagining department ever since he used it all up building Lady B her dream getaway. Fortunately, *I* still have enough imagination to go around – without it, you two would be dino-dinner…"

"Puffwinkles! I had everything in key-fingered hand," insisted Skeleton Keys. "And there would not have been any trouble if not for your insidious imagining!"

"I don't know if you've been paying attention, funny fingers, but the Kingdom only allows *good imaginings*," ImagiNathan replied. He effortlessly conjured a replacement pram for Daisy (this time in blue and white stripes) and pushed it over to Skeleton Keys, who lowered Daisy inside. "Rules are rules," added ImagiNathan. "There's no way I could have dreamed up this daft dino even if I wanted to."

"Dreamed up...?" Lucky whispered to himself. He pulled Stanley's sketchbook out of his pouch and leafed through the pages. After several pages of bees, Lucky fell upon a drawing of a scaly, savage dinosaur, standing on a rock and roaring in rage. He glanced over at ImagiNathan's thought bubble and realized the drawing looked exactly like the creature trapped inside it.

A wild thought entered Lucky's head.

Did Stanley imagine the diner-saur?

"M-Mr Keys," said Lucky, trembling as he held up the book. "*Look.*"

"Not now, figment, I am giving this figswindler a piece of my mind," hissed Skeleton Keys.

"Your mind couldn't imagine its way out of a wet paper bag, funny fingers," laughed ImagiNathan.

"But Mr Keys—" Lucky said again.

"And if anyone can find a way around the Rule of Good Imagining, it is *you*!" Skeleton Keys cried.

"Why would I imagine a dinosaur just to trap it in my *inescapa-bubble*?" scoffed ImagiNathan, prodding the sphere again.

"Because you are nothing but—"

"*Mr Keys!*"

Finally, Skeleton Keys turned to see Lucky holding Stanley's sketchbook aloft.

"It's Stanley," he said. "He's imagine-ding, look! I think he imagine-did that diner—"

POP!

Everyone froze. ImagiNathan saw a look of horror spread across Lucky's face. Then he felt the heat from a growling breath, and turned.

The dinosaur was free.

"AAaaAAaAH!" ImagiNathan screeched as the dinosaur swatted him through the air with its great, scaly tail. Then in a swift blur of movement it charged, pouncing on Lucky and pinning him to the ground with a huge claw.

"Figment!" Skeleton Keys cried. He immediately leaped on to the dinosaur's back and flung his bony arms around its neck. The lizard thrashed, bucking the skeleton and sending him flying through the air.

Lucky tried to scream but his own fear silenced the cry. The dinosaur glowered down at him, teeth bared. Then it paused. Lucky felt the creature's hot breath puffing on to his face as it looked at him. For a moment, Lucky thought he saw a flash of recognition in the dinosaur's glowing red eyes, almost as if it knew him.

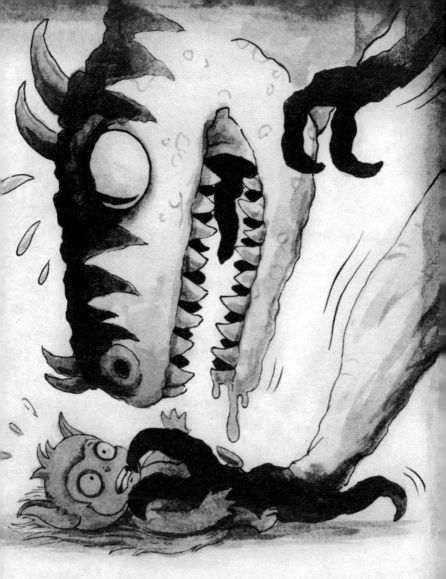

"Have – have you seen Stanley?" Lucky whimpered.

Then the dinosaur vanished into thin air.

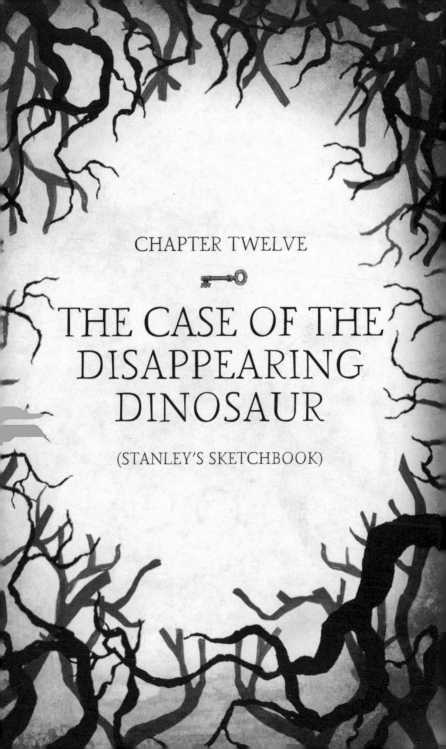

CHAPTER TWELVE

THE CASE OF THE DISAPPEARING DINOSAUR

(STANLEY'S SKETCHBOOK)

The 1st Rule of the Kingdom:
NO HUMANS ALLOWED
The 2nd Rule of the Kingdom:
GOOD IMAGININGS ONLY

Lucky sat up with a start. The dinosaur was nowhere to be seen.

"Heck and high water!" ImagiNathan shrieked, picking up his top hat and dusting it off. "Where'd the dino go?"

"Do not try and pull the wool over my eye sockets, Nathan," protested Skeleton Keys, rubbing his head as he got to his feet. "This is exactly the chaos you crave. I am only surprised Milady has not seen through you."

"Seen through me? She can barely take her eyes off me," said ImagiNathan, pushing his hat on to his head with a smug grin. "Now in case you've forgotten, Lady B chose me to find the little cantaloupe's human – so why don't you stay out of trouble long enough for me to do my job?"

A BLOOOF! of blinding red smoke later, and ImagiNathan had vanished, leaving Lucky staring down at Stanley's drawing of a dinosaur.

"Scammering, rottering rugslugger..." growled Skeleton Keys, checking on Daisy as she snored softly in the pram. "Trust Nathan to find a way to break the rules! I knew it was a mistake bringing him to the Kingdom..."

"But it wasn't him, Mr Keys, it was Stanley!" Lucky cried, hopping after him and waving Stanley's sketchbook. "He drew a diner-saur just like it in his doodle diary, look!"

Skeleton Keys glanced back at the drawing.

"Why, 'tis a fair likeness, to be sure," he

admitted, scratching his head with a key-tipped finger. "I suppose it is *possible* that a human in the Kingdom could create imaginings too. Theirs are the wildest imaginations of all! But—"

"Maybe Stanley sent his imagine-ding to find us! Maybe he's trying to biggin *tell* us something," continued Lucky. "What if we're looking for him, but he's looking for us too?"

"By imagining that scaly savage to attack us? Cheese 'n' biscuits! If that is his idea of friendship, then Stanley Strange is not the friend you imagine!" Skeleton Keys started to push the pram down the street.

"Mark my words, figment – the dinosaur was clearly *ImagiNathan's* work. He has found a way to break the rules and bring his bothersome brand of maddening mayhem to the Kingdom! But if *I* find Stanley Strange before him, I shall puncture his plans and prove to Lady Byrd – as if such a thing needs proving – that he is no competition for Ol' Mr Keys..."

Lucky wasn't sure he really understood what the skeleton was saying, but in the end, all he could really think about was the dinosaur. It *had* to be Stanley's imagining.

"Don't stop imagine-ding, Stanley..." Lucky whispered, and returned the sketchbook to his pouch. Then he realized Skeleton Keys had sped away down the street, and hopped after him.

Lucky followed Skeleton Keys through the Kingdom as he continued his frantic search for Stanley Strange, determined to find him before ImagiNathan. From the top to the bottom of the hill, from one corner of the Kingdom to the other, until the sun began its slow descent towards the horizon. It felt like they had searched every nook and cranny and knocked on every door. But no one – from Big-Head Fred to Unicorn Hedgehog to Six-Armed Saoirse to Fart Pig – not one unimaginary had even seen Lucky's best friend.

By sunset, there was nowhere left to search. Skeleton Keys and Lucky found themselves back at the beach.

"Of all the confuddlements! I hope ImagiNathan has had no more luck," grumbled Skeleton Keys, trying with some difficulty to push Daisy's pram over the pebbles. "How does Stanley Strange stay unfound and unnoticed? Someone *must* have let him into the Kingdom. Who opened the door, and bones 'n' buckles, why?"

"I just hope he's OK," said Lucky. "We've never been apart before. Not being with him feels like I'm not the whole me. I don't know what to—"

A distant booming interrupted Lucky's train of thought. He turned his ear back to the village, the booming growing louder by the moment.

"Dogs 'n' cats, what is that racket?" said Skeleton Keys.

"Something's coming ... something biggin *big*," Lucky whispered, the now ground-shaking BOOM BOOM BOOM echoing around the Kingdom. Suddenly, Lucky caught sight of a huge shape moving between two of the taller houses. Though it was partly concealed by the buildings in front of it,

Lucky could see it was as tall as the houses themselves. Its thunderous footsteps made the buildings, trees and lampposts shudder. Finally, it emerged from the village on to the edge of the beach.

It was a vast, metal figure, ten metres tall, with a tubular body and long legs that whirred and clanked as it walked. Its head was a gleaming metal dome, with a single bright searchlight for an eye. The blinding-white beam scanned the street below, illuminating villagers who gazed up in excitement at this new visitor.

"Crumcrinkles," Skeleton Keys whispered. "What...?"

"It's a *robot*," Lucky gasped, peering wide-eyed at the metal giant. He pulled Stanley's sketchbook out of his pouch and flicked through to the centre pages. There it was – a drawing of a giant, gleaming robot, towering menacingly over a city and looking for all the world like the one now stomping through the Kingdom. "Mr Keys, it's Stanley's robot!" Lucky cried, holding out the book. "He's imagine-ding again!"

"Pifflechips – that gear-filled Goliath has ImagiNathan written all over it," Skeleton Keys insisted as, with a loud hum of transistors, the robot turned back and made its way into the village. "Let us just hope that chaotic conjuror does not intend for his imagining to break the rules again…"

As if on cue, the metal Titan lifted a long metal arm and swung it at the nearest house, smashing its roof and sending shattered tiles and bricks crashing to the ground below.

"No!" Lucky cried.

"Crumcrinkles! That robotic rumbleshover is not so much breaking the rules as obliterating them – come on, figment," Skeleton Keys said, pushing the pram back up the beach as fast as he could. "ImagiNathan has gone too far this time, but if it is a fight he wants, then by my bones 'tis a fight he will get!"

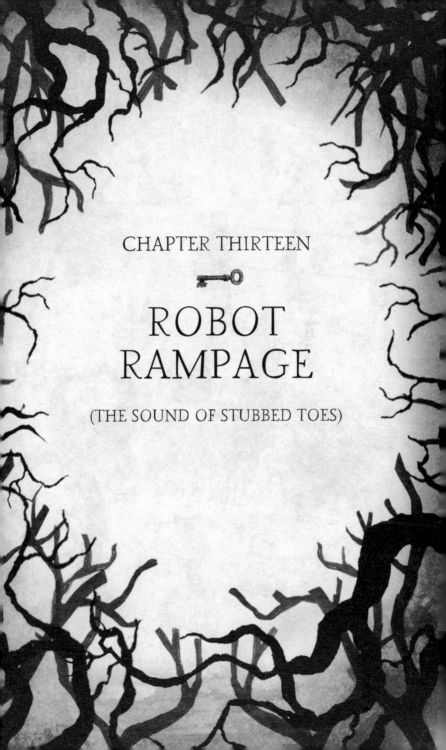

CHAPTER THIRTEEN

ROBOT
RAMPAGE

(THE SOUND OF STUBBED TOES)

*UNIMAGINARY GIANTS, TITANS,
BEHEMOTHS AND/OR COLLOSI*
(An Incomplete List)
1. Atlas 2. Goliath 3. Bigfoot 4. Little John 5. Jolly Green

W ith the sound of the robot's booming footsteps echoing in their ears, Lucky and the pram-pushing Skeleton Keys followed the trail of destruction through the village.

"Why would Stanley imagine a rampage-ding robot?" Lucky asked, struggling to keep up with the skeleton's strides. "Why doesn't he just say hello?"

"Do not be foolboozled, figment! This is ImagiNathan's work, I would bet my bones on it," replied the skeleton as screaming unimaginaries hurried in the opposite direction. "I must dispatch that mechanical menace before it does any more damage..."

They rounded a corner into a wide courtyard surrounded by houses, shops and museums, and with a grand fountain in its centre. Towering over even the tallest building in the square was the robot. With a swing of its arm, it obliterated the entire wall of a house in an instant, to reveal Unicorn Hedgehog reading a book on the toilet. Then it tore the roof off a charming pottery shop (the long-time dream of Banana with Two Faces) and flung the debris through the air.

"Every banana for themselves!" screamed both of Banana with Two Faces' faces as she fled the crumbling shop.

"Figment, take Daisy and get to cover," instructed Skeleton Keys, pushing the pram over to Lucky.

"W-what are you going to do?" Lucky asked,

using all his strength to drag the pram behind a half-shattered wall in a corner of the courtyard.

"Save the day, of course!" cried the skeleton. "This calls for the *Key to*—"

BLOOOF!

A puff of red smoke exploded on the other side of the courtyard. Skeleton Keys let out a rattling sigh of frustration as, an instant later, ImagiNathan emerged.

"Funny fingers! Heck and high water, what's all this?" he bellowed, gazing in horror at the unfolding chaos.

"Do not play dumbfounded with me, you insidious imaginer!" Skeleton Keys replied, before wiggling one of his key-tipped fingers. "Well, Ol' Mr Keys has a trick or two, too! For anything is possible when the *Key to Possibility* makes anything possible ... possibly."

From his cover behind the wall, Lucky watched Skeleton Keys stride to the nearest door. He thrust the key into the lock and turned it with a CLICK CLUNK.

"Unreasonably unrestrained robot, behold the power of anything is possible-ness!" the skeleton shouted and swung open the door.

"Oww! Ow! Ouch!"

As pained cries rang out, Skeleton Keys and Lucky peered inside. The room was an abyss of light-swallowing darkness, populated only by the uncomfortable grunts coming from inside.

"Oof! Yow! OW!"

"Uhh, what is it, Mr Keys?" Lucky called out.

"That … is the sound of stubbed toes," said Skeleton Keys, trying to hide his disappointment.

"Owie! Argh! Owww!"

"Stubbed … toes?" repeated Lucky.

"The *Key to Possibility* makes *anything* possible," he reiterated with a slight shake of his head. "Today, it has made it possible for the sound of every stubbed toe ever to exist behind this door."

"OUCH! Ooo! Yowch! Ow!"

"Is – is that going to help us stop the giant robot?" Lucky asked hopefully.

"It is not," admitted Skeleton Keys, pushing the door closed.

"Is that all you've got, funny fingers?" ImagiNathan hollered from the other side of the courtyard. "Well, stand back and let Lady B's number one unimaginary handle—"

The robot's arm moved so fast, ImagiNathan didn't even see it coming. It swatted the building above him, sending a cascade of rubble tumbling down. In seconds, ImagiNathan was buried beneath a mountain of debris.

"Nathan!" Skeleton Keys cried as the robot drew back one of its vast, metal feet. With a swift kick, it sent the skeleton flying across the square. He crashed limply into a broken wall with a clatter of dry bones – before the wall fell on top of him.

"Mr Keys!" Lucky cried out. He glanced into the pram at Daisy, hoping that she'd begun to stir. But the girl with the backwards head slept on. Then he looked back and saw the robot drive its foot into a pastel pink building (proudly bearing the sign *Fart Pig's Toot-tacular Gallery of Fart Art*) and crush it like a cardboard box.

Lucky couldn't understand why his best friend would imagine anything as bad as this, but the robot showed no sign of stopping its rampage. He had to do something.

Lucky found himself hopping out from behind the wall.

"Stop!" he cried from below. He took a nervous step backwards. "Please, Stanley's robot, stop!"

The robot lifted both of its arms to smash yet another house to dust, when it suddenly paused, the whirring and clanking of its limbs giving way to an eerie quiet (apart from the panicked screams of fleeing unimaginaries). At last, its head swivelled to face Lucky, looming over him and bathing him in stark, white light.

"My name's Lucky and I'm sort of one of Stanley's imagine-dings too," Lucky called out. The robot's searchlight eye seemed to dim a little. Then it lifted a great foot, its shadow falling over Lucky.

Stanley Strange's unimaginary friend closed his eyes. "Please don't stomp on me," he pleaded. "I just want to biggin find Stanley, that's all."

There was a pause. Lucky opened one eye to see the robot lower its foot to the ground. It turned away, the light from its eye suddenly focused into a searing beam that streaked over the village.

Lucky squinted, following the beam across the sky. It was illuminating a distant house at the very top of the hill.

Lady Byrd's atrium.

"Milady Byrd's house?" Lucky muttered. "I don't get what—"

The light suddenly faded, and Lucky turned to see that the robot had evaporated – disappeared into nothingness.

"Wait!" he cried. "Don't go!"

Lucky scratched the back of his head. First the dinosaur, then the robot. He took Stanley's sketchbook out of his pouch, leafing past pictures of bees, then dinosaurs, then robots. He kept turning. On the last page, the drawing covered both pages – a dozen huge, saucer-shaped spaceships descending over a city. Rays of searing energy blasted out from coiled cannons, reducing the city to atoms.

"Stanley, maybe you should stop imagine-ding..." Lucky whispered. Then:

"*Lucky...*"

Lucky could have sworn someone said his name. He turned and stared into the gloom of an alleyway behind him. A figure stood in the shadows. At first, Lucky didn't believe what he was seeing – so many impossible things had happened since he had arrived in the Kingdom that he barely trusted his own senses any more. He blinked and narrowed his eyes. The figure raised an arm, beckoning him closer. Lucky took a single step forward. The figure did the same, moving into the warm, yellowish light of the last working street light in the square.

Lucky's jaw fell open.

It was Stanley.

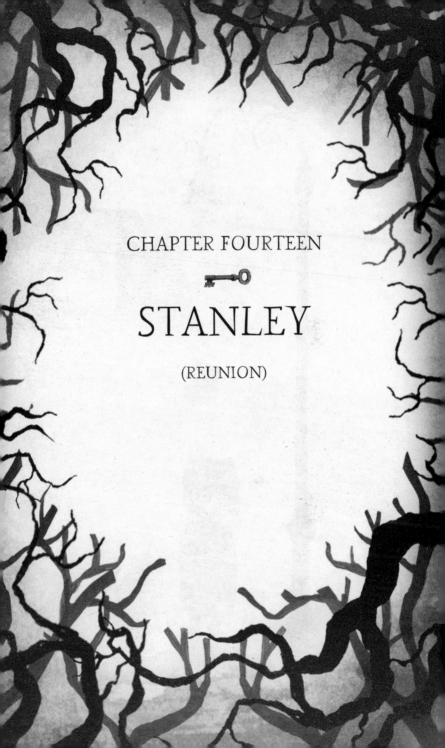

CHAPTER FOURTEEN

STANLEY

(REUNION)

"A friend is a friend 'til the very end!
But, for an unimaginary, the end is just the beginning..."
—SK

"S-Stanley...?"

There was no doubt. There was his best friend, complete with his big coat and round glasses and striped beanie hat, smiling a wide, excited smile. Lucky broke into a half run, half hop, racing towards Stanley so fast he almost tripped over his own legs. He flung his arms around him. "Stanley!" Lucky said, trapping his friend in an inescapable hug. "Where've you biggin been?"

"I was hiding," Stanley said with a half laugh, half wheeze. "Sorry, Lucky, I didn't mean to scare you..."

"You're like a biggin million ninjas! We couldn't find you *anywhere*," Lucky declared, finally releasing him from his hug and wiping a happy tear from his eye. "I wasn't *never* going to give up on finding you, even though all I found was your wild imagine-dings..."

"Don't worry about all that," Stanley said. "But we need to get out of here."

"Shouldn't we check on Mr Keys? That robot biggin booted him!" Lucky said, looking back at the courtyard. "He's a skelly-ton with keys on his finger-trips and he found me and he's been helping me look for you and there's this girl called Daisy and Milady Byrd put her to sleep and then—"

"Lucky, *listen* to me," said Stanley. "We need to leave, right away."

"What?" said Lucky. "But Mr Keys—"

"You do trust me, don't you, Lucky?"

Stanley asked.

"Of course I biggin trust you. You're my biggin best friend in all the world, Stanley."

Stanley put both hands on Lucky's shoulders. "Then let's go."

"Go? Where?"

"To the Exit," Stanley said. "We're going home."

Lucky was desperate to check on Skeleton Keys, but Stanley had already started to make his way down the alleyway towards the beach. There was no way Lucky was going to lose him again. With a final glance towards the square, he hopped after his friend.

Stanley was running by now, and Lucky had to redouble his hopping pace to keep up. The pair ran through the village, following the robot's trail of destruction in reverse until they emerged at the beach. As Stanley hurried on to the pebbles, Lucky remembered

Stanley's sketchbook. He took it out of his pouch and held it out. "Stanley, wait! I've been keeping it safe for you. I knew when I saw your diner-saur you were trying to find me with your imagine-dings."

"Keep it," Stanley said, making a beeline for the Exit door.

"Oh ... OK," Lucky replied, pocketing the
book again. "So, why did you imagine biggin
bad imagine-dings?" he asked as Stanley
grabbed the door handle. "I mean, if you
wanted me to find you, why not imagine
good imagine-dings?"

Stanley pulled open the door without answering. While night had fallen in the Kingdom, bright sunshine poured in from the other side.

"Go on, Lucky," Stanley said. "I'll be right behind you."

Lucky looked back once more at the village, a pang of guilt twisting in his gut at abandoning Skeleton Keys.

"I don't—"

"I told you to trust me," Stanley said. "I'm your best friend, aren't I?"

Lucky paused, just for a moment – but he'd just got his best friend back and he wasn't about to argue. He stepped through the door. The green hills and blue skies of the real world were bright, and the afternoon air was crisp and welcoming.

"Do you think we'll come back to the Kingdom, Stanley?" he asked.

"No, you're never coming back," replied Stanley from the other side of the door. "Stanley knows best."

Then he slammed the door in Lucky's face.

CHAPTER FIFTEEN

SHUT OUT

(STANLEY VS DAISY)

From *The Important Thoughts of Mr S. Keys,*
Volume 12: Doors

A door is never just a door!
Except for when it is.

"Stanley? What's happening?" Lucky
cried. He raced to the door and banged
on it. "Stanley! Open the biggin door!"

Instinctively, Lucky grabbed the door
handle and turned. The door swung open and
Lucky all but fell through. But he did not find
himself back in the Kingdom. He was just on
the other side of a door to nowhere. Still on
the hill – still in the real world. "Stanley!"
Lucky shouted again, racing round to the
other side and pulling the door shut. "Stanley,
please open the door! It's me, Lucky!"

Lucky banged on the door one more time. He took a step back and waited. He stared at the handle, willing it to turn – but the Exit remained firmly shut. He was trapped in the real world, with no way of getting back to his friend.

Lucky's mind raced. Why would Stanley lock him out? He suddenly remembered what Skeleton Keys had said after the dinosaur attack:

"If that is his idea of friendship, then Stanley Strange is not the friend you imagine..."

Lucky hadn't even entertained the idea, but it was suddenly all he could think about.

What if Stanley didn't want to be friends any more?

Lucky slumped to his knees as tears dampened the fur on his cheeks. Stanley was all he had ever had. Now he had no one. He'd never felt more alone.

"Get back here, you tangerine!"

Lucky spun round to see the door swing open. Even in the Kingdom's fading light, he could see Stanley in the doorway, doing a sort of odd, writhing dance. He didn't look at all happy.

"Stanley!" Lucky cried. "I knew it was a mistake! I knew you wasn't going to ad-bandon me!"

"Get off me!" Stanley growled.

"Stanley...?" Lucky uttered as he hopped towards the door. He'd almost reached it when the squirming Stanley grabbed the handle and tried to pull the door shut again. In an instant, Daisy appeared on Stanley's back. Her arms were wrapped around the boy's neck.

"*Daisy?* You're awake!" gasped Lucky, pushing the door open and hopping back through. "Daisy, stop, that's Stanley!"

"So? He shut you out, you soppy satsuma!"
Daisy snarled, hanging off Stanley's back as he
spun round, desperately trying to throw her
to the ground. "Now get over here and stamp
on his toes!"

"Don't listen to her, Lucky!" Stanley
pleaded. "Help me!"

"But—" Lucky uttered.

"I'm your best friend, Lucky! Help!" Stanley barked, thrashing about as Daisy tightened her grip around his neck. "Get her off!"

"'Stanley knows best'..." Lucky muttered.

"What?" Stanley and Daisy shouted at once. Lucky held his hand to his mouth, Stanley's words echoing in his brain. He stared at his 'friend' as if suddenly seeing him for the first time.

"You said, 'Stanley knows best'," he said. "Stanley wouldn't say that."

Stanley stopped struggling.

An instant later, he vanished.

Daisy fell to the ground with a clatter of pebbles.

"Stanley!" Lucky cried.

"If that was your friend, then so am I. And I'm not," said Daisy, dusting herself off. "That was just another stupid imagining."

"An *imagine-ding*? B-but I gave him my biggin best hug..." Lucky sniffed. He stood there for a moment in the gloom, not quite able to believe what had happened. He bent down and picked up a pebble where the imagined Stanley had stood moments ago. "I really biggin thought it was him," he said with a sniff.

"Start crying again and I'll shove you out of that door myself," grunted Daisy as she got to her feet. "You think you've got problems? I woke up in a *pram*. Nobody tells me when it's nap time! Bugatha's gone straight to the top of my revenge list..."

"Biggin *loads* has happened since you were sing-did to sleep," said Lucky. "There was this red magician and this diner-saur and this giant robot and—"

"Ugh, I missed a giant robot? Stupid Bugatha," Daisy growled. "All I saw was you running off with your bestest fake friend in the whole world. I know when something doesn't smell right and that was *stinky*, so I followed you. Now where's bone-bag? I need to tell him I saved the day again."

"Mr Keys? Stanley's biggin robot got him!" said Lucky, remembering the carnage left in the courtyard. "He got bumped into a wall and buried! Daisy, we have to go biggin back!"

"I'm never *not* saving that bag of bones from something or other," sighed Daisy, and kicked the Exit door shut with her foot. Immediately, the message they heard when they first entered the Kingdom began to play.

"Greetings! Welcome to the Kingdom. We are so happy you have decided to join us..."

"Ugh, I wish she'd shut *up*," snarled Daisy, clenching her fists.

"Not before a little song..." said a voice.

Lucky spun round to see a figure step out from behind the Exit door. Even in the gloom, he recognized her immediately.

It was Lady Byrd.

"It – it was you, wasn't it, Milady Byrd?" Lucky said. "*You* imagine-did Stanley."

Lady Byrd gave a shrug, her insect eyes unblinking.

"What can I say?" she said at last. "Lady Byrd knows best."

CHAPTER SIXTEEN

LADY BYRD'S CONFESSION

(HE SLEEPS)

"There is nothing so real
As that which we feel."
—SK

"You put me to sleep, Bugatha," Daisy growled as Lady Byrd began edging towards them. "That makes you Daisy Enemy Number One."

"That nap doesn't seem to have improved your mood," Lady Byrd said, moving closer. "Perhaps you could do with another."

"Why did you imagine Stanley?" Lucky blurted, his voice cracking with emotion. "'Good imagine-dings only', you said!"

"It *was* good – for the good of the Kingdom," hissed Lady Byrd.

"But how do you even know what Stanley looked like? You've never even … met … him…" Lucky trailed off, the realization taking his breath away. "You *have* met him, haven't you?" he whispered, his eyes wide. "On the hill. It was you in the doorway. *You* opened the door."

"You've had a long day, child," Lady Byrd said, leaning closer. "Everything will seem better after a nice, long sleep…"

"Don't you dare—!" was all Daisy could get out before Lady Byrd unleashed her strange, whistling Byrd Song. Lucky felt the hum in his bones and drowsiness overcame him in an instant. He turned to see Daisy rocking woozily on her feet as he felt his eyelids begin to close…

"Milady!"

The cry cut Lady Byrd off mid-song. Lucky felt as if someone had suddenly shaken him awake. He turned to see Skeleton Keys limping down the beach, his clothes torn and covered in brick dust, and propping up an even more battered ImagiNathan.

"M-Mr Keys! ImagiNathan!" Lady Byrd shrieked. "How wonderful to see my two favourite—"

"Save it, Bugatha, you're *rumbled*," snapped Daisy, kicking pebbles in Lady Byrd's direction. "Turns out your precious Lady Byrd is behind it all, bone-bag," she told Skeleton Keys. "You just missed her imagining a fake Stanley Strange for the mango here."

"Imagining?" wheezed ImagiNathan. "I'm confused – I thought the little cantaloupe's friend was human."

"Milady...?" Skeleton Keys knocked brick dust out of his earhole, not quite able to believe what he was hearing. "Is this true? Did you imagine this figment's friend?"

Of – of course not!" Lady Byrd said. "Mr Keys, your partner is not only rude but a liar to boot!"

"Daisy is many troublesome things, but a fibbing figswindler is not one of them," Skeleton Keys insisted. "Which leaves me with a most confuddling question, Milady – why?"

Lady Byrd glanced over at Lucky, and for a moment it looked as if she might take to the air. At last she shook her head slowly, sadly, and let out a long, defeated sigh.

"I knew you would never stop looking for your friend," she told Lucky quietly. "I had to get you out. Imagining the human was the only way."

"Where is he? Where's Stanley?" Lucky said, as firmly as he'd said anything. "Tell me!"

"Safe, where he belongs," she said. "Lady Byrd knows best..."

"Not this time, Milady," said Skeleton Keys.

"Dogs 'n' cats, how could you?"

"Yeah, you broke your own rule, Bugatha," said Daisy. "No Humans Allowed."

"You wouldn't understand! None of you would!" cried Lady Byrd. "I've been in the Kingdom for a hundred years. Everything is imagined. But out there, beyond the Exit – that is real. I-I started to *miss* it..."

"If you wanted to go back to the real world, Milady, you could have returned at any time," said Skeleton Keys.

"And leave my Kingdom? Never!" Lady Byrd protested. "Yet I would go to the Exit, just to peek out – just to see the real world again. It was enough ... until today. Today, when I opened the door, I saw *him*. He was sitting there, drawing."

"Stanley?" Lucky whispered.

"He looked so like the boy who imagined me," Lady Byrd admitted. "It was as if he'd come back to me, after all that time. And he was *real*. I don't know what came over me, but before I knew it I had sung him to sleep ... and brought him here."

"And no one would have been any the wiser, had Stanley not unimagined his IF in the moment he fell into slumber," said Skeleton Keys, piecing the mystery together.

"A friend whom Stanley knew would never give up looking for him."

"Wait, is that why we couldn't find the mango's friend? 'Cause he's *asleep*?" Daisy huffed, throwing her arms up. "That stupid song is your answer to everything, Bugatha."

"But Stanley can't be asleep," Lucky said, scratching his head. "He's imagine-ding. He imagine-did that robot!"

"That mechanical menace in the courtyard?" said Lady Byrd. "That was ImagiNathan's work, wasn't it?"

"Heck and high water, why does everyone always blame me?" said ImagiNathan, coughing up a bit of brick as Skeleton Keys set him down on the pebbles.

"You've been trying to break the rules of the Kingdom since you got here, ImagiNathan," Lady Byrd said. "I knew if I pitted you against Mr Keys, you'd both make a lot of noise and never get anywhere in your search."

"I too was foolsome enough to believe Nathan was the cause of the Kingdom's calamity – until that rumbleshoving robot buried him beneath a building!" explained Skeleton Keys. He brushed the dust from both shoulders and pointed a key-tipped finger at Lucky. "'Twas only then that I realized that this poor figment was right all along – Stanley Strange is *imagining*."

"Imagine-ding his *doodles*," added Lucky, taking the sketchbook out of his pouch. He handed it to Lady Byrd and the book fell open at a drawing of a monstrous dinosaur.

"The human – Stanley drew these?" she said, turning to a picture of a towering robot.

"Stanley's biggin best at drawing, but his imagine-dings are real now," said Lucky. Lady Byrd turned to the last pages – Stanley's drawing of spaceships laying waste to a city.

"That sketchbook may be a prophecy of things to come," warned Skeleton Keys. "Stanley is imagining, and his imaginings are growing wilder by the hour."

"But it cannot be," said Lady Byrd with a shake of her head. "He sleeps."

"He dreams!" Skeleton Keys cried. "Do you not see, Milady? That is why his imaginings are so untamed, coming and going with the fretful cycles of sleep! Stanley Strange can no more choose his dreams than control his wild imaginings. They are not tied 'n' tethered to the rules. We must wake him up, before—"

"Uh, bone-bag?" said Daisy, gazing up as an eerie greenish light fell over the beach. "Here we go again..."

Lucky followed Daisy's gaze up. A huge, saucer-shaped object had appeared in the sky. The silvery spinning saucer hovered, humming, over the village.

"Dogs 'n' cats!" cried Skeleton Keys as a second, third and fourth flying saucer materialized in the sky. "'Tis an invasion!"

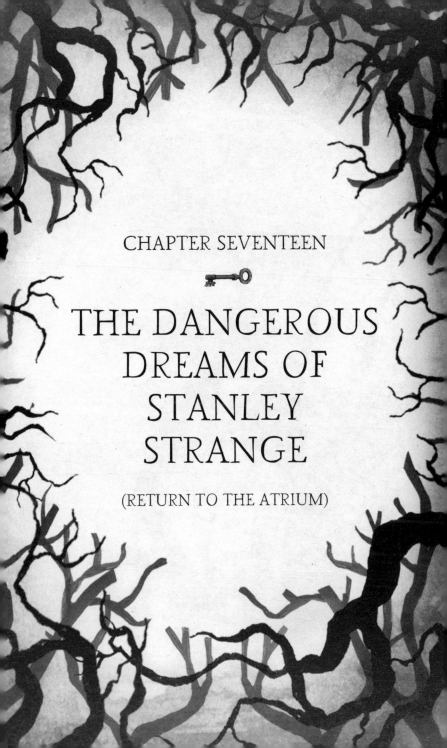

CHAPTER SEVENTEEN

THE DANGEROUS DREAMS OF STANLEY STRANGE

(RETURN TO THE ATRIUM)

I never quite know where I stand
Will Daisy vex, or lend a hand?
Will she save me from a world of trouble
Or, if she fancies, burst my bubble?

"We must awaken Stanley Strange, before his dreams destroy the Kingdom," said Skeleton Keys. "Tell us, Milady – where is he?"

Lady Byrd peered up at the flying saucers appearing in the sky, and then down at Stanley's drawing of the same spaceships destroying a city.

"He's in the atrium," she confessed. "Asleep, in the top of the tree."

"Ugh, was he there all along?" Daisy groaned. "You're *really* getting on my bad side, Bugatha."

Lady Byrd lowered her head with a sigh as Lucky peered up into the darkening sky. The flying saucers now numbered six. They had begun to circle the Kingdom.

"Biggin loads of 'em," he whispered. "What if we can't get there in time?"

"Fret not," declared Skeleton Keys. "Between my fantabulant fingers and a door or twelve, I shall get us to—"

"*I'll* get you there," said ImagiNathan, still sprawled on the beach. With a BOIP! a single large thought bubble formed around Skeleton Keys, Lady Byrd, Daisy and Lucky.

"Bones 'n' buckles!" cried Skeleton Keys as the sphere began to float up into the air. "Quick-thinking, Nathan!"

"For the last time, it's ImagiNathan!" shouted ImagiNathan after them, but the incredible orb had already drifted high into the sky.

The thought bubble floated over the Kingdom, rising over rooftops and up and up, until it passed between the strange, silvery saucers.

"Even biggin *more* of 'em," whispered Lucky. By now, the spaceships numbered an even dozen – the same number as in Stanley's sketchbook.

"Can these really be wild imaginings of one human?" asked Lady Byrd, peering out of the thought bubble.

"Yeah, but if you look *really* closely," began Daisy, "you can see that it's all your stupid fault."

A shrieking whirr suddenly echoed through the air. Skeleton Keys pressed his face against the elastic sphere. One after the other, he saw the fleet of flying saucers deploy long, coiled cannons, which glowed and pulsed with destructive power.

"Dogs 'n' cats..." he said in an urgent whisper. "The invaders have powered up their cannons – 'tis the beginning of the end!"

"At least we've got a good view," said Daisy with a shrug.

Skeleton Keys glanced down between his feet. The atrium was now directly below them – and they were about to float right over it.

"Cheese 'n' biscuits, we're still climbing!" said Skeleton Keys. "Descend, you befuddling bubble, descend!"

"Shut up, bone-bag, I'm trying to think," Daisy said. Lucky turned to see her scrunching up her face. After a moment, she held up her finger and thumb, pressed tightly together.

"Daisy?" Skeleton Keys began suspiciously. "What are you doing?"

"I'm *imagining*, obviously," she said with gritted teeth.

A moment later, Lucky saw it. Pressed between her fingers was a tiny pin.

"*Finally*," she said, her eyes wild.

"No biggin way," Lucky muttered.

"Crumcrinkles, Daisy, you had better not be

thinking what I think you are thinking,"
said a fretful Skeleton Keys. "We are too high!
Do not—!"

But it was too late.

Daisy jabbed the pin into the thought
bubble.

POP!

CHAPTER EIGHTEEN

FOUND

(WAKE UP, STANLEY STRANGE)

> *"'Tis when I plummet through the sky,*
> *I tend to wish that I could fly."*
> —*SK*

L ucky realized he was in thin air and
falling for the second time that day. After
Daisy popped the thought bubble, he,
Skeleton Keys, Lady Byrd and, of course, Daisy
fell towards the atrium. It was only when
Lucky didn't collide with its glass roof that he
looked up.

Lady Byrd had him, caught in one of her
hook-like feet. In the other, she had Daisy,
and held Skeleton Keys safely in her arms. Her
wings beat in a swift blur of movement as she
lowered them through the sky.

"This doesn't mean all is forgiven, Bugatha," grunted Daisy.

"Daisy, that pin – you *imagine-did*," said Lucky as he dangled. "You imagine-did a good imagine-ding!"

"Good...?" Daisy whispered, and glowered at Lucky. "If you tell anyone – *anyone* – I'll pop you next, Stan-fan."

Lady Byrd deposited the trio on to the domed roof of the atrium and Lucky found his face pressed against the glass. He could see the top of the tree just below, stretching almost as high as the dome itself. Then he spotted something that made his heart skip a beat – a figure, lying upon a tightly knotted cradle of branches and leaves, and dressed in a big coat and striped beanie hat.

Lucky turned to Lady Byrd.

"Milady Byrd?" he whimpered, his breath fogging his view as he tapped lightly on the glass. "Is he an imagine-ding?"

"No, child," declared Lady Byrd with a sigh. "That is your friend. That's Stanley Strange."

"About time too," tutted Daisy. She stuck the pin into the roof and with another POP! the glass vanished, dropping them on to the nest of branches beside the sleeping Stanley. "I'm getting good at this," Daisy noted, scowling at Lady Byrd. "Next time, I'm going to stick this pin in your—"

"Stanley! It's me, it's Lucky!" Lucky cried, taking his friend by the shoulders. "Wake up, Stanley, I found you ... and I've been looking for you biggin everywhere."

"The invaders have stopped multiplying – it is surely only moments before the prophecy of Stanley's doodled doomsday comes to pass," said Skeleton Keys, glancing skywards. "Wake him up, Milady – hurry!"

"Me, wake him? Is that your plan? Why

didn't you tell me?" she said, her insect eyes flashing with dread. "My song was powerful – I could not risk him waking in the Kingdom. He will sleep for days ... perhaps weeks!"

"Wait, you *can't wake him*? Silly, stupid Bugatha, why do you think we brought you along?" growled Daisy. "Argh, that's it! I'm going to stick so many pins in you, you won't be able to drink without leaking!"

"You need to wake up, Stanley," Lucky whispered as Stanley's neck lolled back. "You're dreaming up imagine-dings and your imagine-dings are *bad*."

As if on cue, the sky lit up with a blinding green light. High above them, rays streaked out from the barrels of the flying saucers. In a single, horrifying moment, a dozen houses were disintegrated. No brick was left un-vaporized – they were blasted to nothingness, as if they had never even existed.

"The ending has begun, dallywanglers," Skeleton Keys uttered as more and more rays streaked towards the ground. "Stanley Strange's imaginings are destroying the Kingdom."

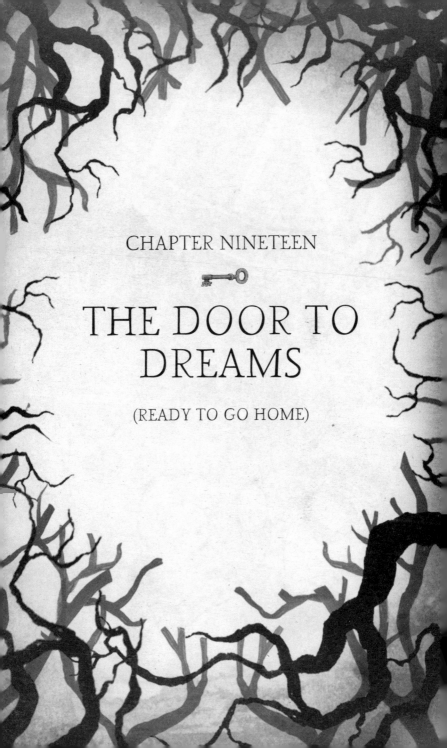

CHAPTER NINETEEN

THE DOOR TO DREAMS

(READY TO GO HOME)

From *The Important Thoughts of Mr S. Keys,*
Volume 6: The Key to Imagination

'Tis the key to my most favourite place!
But where does it lead? I cannot imagine!

Lucky held his best friend in his arms as
the flying saucers unleashed another
barrage of searing rays. They lit up the
darkness, reducing more of the Kingdom to
atoms.

"Stupid End of the World," Daisy huffed.
"Well, let's get it over with – I've got things
to do."

Lucky put his hand on Stanley's arm.

"Please wake up, Stanley," he whispered,
tears dripping on to his friend's coat. "Your
bad dreams are destroying everything to bits."

"Dreams?" Skeleton Keys suddenly blurted. He glanced at his right thumb. "Crumcrinkles, why did I not think of it before?"

"Ugh, could you not have your bright ideas *before* everything goes horribly wrong, bone-bag?" sighed Daisy.

"The *Key to Imagination*," continued the skeleton, the shriek of another ray making the atrium windows shatter. "With it, I can open a door to a world of Stanley Strange's wild imaginings – his imagination itself!"

"Open a door to his imagination? To what end, Mr Keys?" asked Lady Byrd.

"Since he sleeps, the *Key to Imagination* should instead open the door to Stanley's *dreams*," explained Skeleton Keys. "In theory, someone could enter his dreams and rouse him from his slumber."

"Wake him up from inside his own dreams," Lady Byrd mused as more rays streaked towards the Kingdom. "Can it really be done?"

"We can give it a gaddly good go – but we cannot leave the door open for more than a moment," added Skeleton Keys. "If we do not close the door *before* he wakes up, Stanley will remain besnoozed in eternal slumber."

"So, we get in, get him up and get out," said Daisy. "Let's get on with it."

"There is more," added Skeleton Keys gravely. "Whoever enters Stanley's dreams cannot return. In the moment Stanley awakens, they will be trapped inside his dreams for the rest of their days."

"Then I'll go," said Lady Byrd, conjuring a wooden door, not unlike the Exit, in the centre of the cradle of branches. "I am the cause of all this. I must at least try to make it better."

"No, I shall go," replied Skeleton Keys. "It will be a new adventure! After all, Ol' Mr Keys is quite a fan of wild imaginations, even if I do not have one of my—"

"Mr Keys," interrupted Lucky. "It has to be me."

"You? Silly mango – you've only been unimaginary for a day," said Daisy. "You've never even met Stanley for real."

"And if you enter his dreams you never will," Skeleton Keys warned Lucky. "You will have no hope of being unimagined again, figment. You will only be able to meet Stanley in his dreams."

Lucky took a deep breath, and then nodded.

"I'm sorry, child ... for everything," Lady Byrd said. She was hardly able to look at Lucky. "You should not have to pay for my moment of madness."

"It's OK," said Lucky. "Stanley's my biggin

best friend, and that's all that matters. As long as I'm with him, I'm where I belong."

"*No*, you stupid tangerine, don't you get it? *You'll never see him again*," Daisy snarled. "Bone-bag, make Bugatha go..."

"It's OK, Daisy, my biggin mind's made up," Lucky said. He retrieved the sketchbook from his pouch and handed it to her. "Will you give this back to Stanley when he wakes up?"

Daisy said nothing, but took the sketchbook with a huff. Lucky smiled and then turned to Skeleton Keys.

"Are you certain, figment?" the skeleton asked.

"I don't mind saying, I did like being unimagine-dairy," Lucky replied. "But I'm ready to go home now."

Skeleton Keys picked up Stanley in his arms and faced the door. Then he took one of the

boy's hands in his own and put the *Key to Imagination* into the door. It turned with a
CLICK
CLUNK.
"Behold, the door to Stanley's dreams," said the skeleton.

"Thank you, Mr Keys," said Lucky. "Thanks for helping me find Stanley."

Another ray suddenly lit up the night sky, obliterating a nearby house and making the tree shake at its roots. Skeleton Keys looked up to see a flying saucer halt directly in the air above the atrium, its cannons aiming down, ready to fire.

"'Tis now or never, figment!" he said, and swung open the door. Lucky took a deep breath. "Lucky," Skeleton Keys added, "Stanley is fortunate to have you as a friend."

Lucky turned back and smiled.

"I'm lucky too," he said.

Then, as rays streaked towards the atrium,
bathing it in an eerie, neon glow, Lucky
stepped though the doorway and pulled the
door shut.

CHAPTER TWENTY

RETURN TO THE REAL WORLD

(LUCKY YOU)

*Poor Lucky lost his only friend
The Kingdom nearly met its end!
It took a hero, brave and bold
To save the day from threats untold
We honour Lucky's sacrifice
For friendship is a gift for life*

Stanley Strange opened his eyes.

For a moment, he squinted in the blinding green light of the rays, but an instant later, the rays – and the fleet of flying saucers – disappeared.

"Silly satsuma did it," said Daisy, looking up. The sky was dark and serene and dotted with stars.

"Had a weird dream…" began Stanley. He let out a substantial yawn, before looking around in dazed amazement at the skeleton holding him in his arms. He took off his glasses, blinked and put them on again. "Am I still dreaming?"

"Gladdeningly, you are not," said Skeleton Keys, placing the boy on his feet. "Welcome back to the woken world, Stanley Strange. The whats, wherefores and how-did-this-happens are a long and flabbergasting tale, which I will tell you in time. Suffice to say, we owe it all to your imaginary friend."

"Who?" said Stanley, scrunching his face up in confusion. He blinked through sleepy eyes and looked round the gathered unimaginaries, still not sure whether he was seeing what he was seeing. Finally, he fixed his gaze upon Lady Byrd. "I know you..." he muttered. "From the Door to Nowhere."

Lady Byrd could not bring herself to reply. In that moment, she could barely even bring herself to look at Stanley Strange. She turned away, to find Skeleton Keys staring at her.

"I'm sorry, Mr Keys," she said. "Lucky's sacrifice is my responsibility. I will take whatever punishment you see fit to impose."

"You did a foolsome, foulsome thing, Milady, and will have to live with that for the rest of your days ... but perhaps life has already punished you enough," said Skeleton Keys. "I thought the Kingdom would be the solution to your sorrows, but now I believe it is time to give the real world another chance."

"Go back to the real world?" gasped Lady Byrd. "But—"

"I insist, Milady," the skeleton continued. "Who knows? Perhaps the real world will give you another chance too."

"But what about the Kingdom?"

"If today has proved anything, Milady, it is that the Kingdom may finally be better off without you."

"You may be right," Lady Byrd admitted

with a long sigh. "But who is the unimaginary for the job?"

Skeleton Keys rubbed his eye sockets.

"I have a feeling I may regret this..." he said.

"Me, run the Kingdom?" cried ImagiNathan as smoky plumes from his dramatic entrance cleared. Everyone had gathered outside the atrium and, with the ringing of Lady Byrd's summoning bell, ImagiNathan had appeared, still looking a little worse for wear.

"I can hardly believe I am suggesting it, but yes," Skeleton Keys replied.

"I thought I was a rottering rugslugger and a scammering do-no-good," ImagiNathan added with a raise of a red eyebrow.

"Ah, yes, well, perhaps I was a tad hasty in my judgmentals, Nath— *ImagiNathan*," Skeleton Keys confessed.

"Actually, you were dead on the money, funny fingers – I've been nothing but trouble since I got here," said ImagiNathan. "But I don't think I've ever seen *real* trouble until today."

Skeleton Keys peered down the hill. Though much of the Kingdom was devastated by the invasion, the bewildered unimaginaries were already hard at work imagining repairs to their homes.

"A wild imagination can change the world, for better or worse," said the skeleton. "Which will you choose?"

"I'm ImagiNathan," replied the magician with a grin. "I can do anything I put my mind to."

Having placed the Kingdom under ImagiNathan's enthusiastic if unpredictable new management, Skeleton Keys, Daisy and Lady Byrd accompanied Stanley to the Exit door. As the skeleton swung the door open, Lady Byrd took one last look back at the Kingdom.

"Time to face reality, Milady," he said.

"Yes," said Lady Byrd with a nod. "Perhaps it is."

With that, she stepped cautiously through the doorway. Daisy and Stanley followed behind, and finally Skeleton Keys stepped through and pulled the door closed.

It was late afternoon and the hills seemed to gleam in the sunshine. As Lady Byrd took her first tentative steps back in the real world, Daisy turned to Stanley. She held out his sketchbook at arm's length, like it had been dipped in something nasty.

"Yours, I believe," she said.

"Is that my doodle diary?" said Stanley.

"Think of a better name for it, right now,"
Daisy demanded.

"Why do you have it?" Stanley asked,
taking the sketchbook. "I remember I was
sitting drawing and the Door to Nowhere
opened…"

"And blah blah blah, here we are," Daisy
said. "Shut up and look at the last page."

Stanley flipped to the end of the book. On
the inside back cover was a drawing of a stout
orange creature with a blue face, a striped
pouch on his belly and a big, fluffy tail.

"Did you draw this?" Stanley asked. "Who
is it?"

"His name's Lucky," Daisy replied. "You
know him."

"Do I?" said Stanley, staring at the picture.
"I don't remember."

"Lucky you," Daisy said. "Give it time
– you'll see him sooner or later. That silly

satsuma has a habit of getting in your head."

"I-I don't understand," said Stanley.

"Look, I drew you the picture, didn't I?" Daisy huffed. "Just ... don't forget him."

"But what do you—"

"*Every time you go to sleep, think of the stupid tangerine,*" Daisy insisted, glowering at Stanley so intensely that it sent a shudder down his spine. "Promise, or I'll make you sorry you met me."

"I-I promise," Stanley said nervously.

"One never forgets a grinnering good friend! Is that not right, Daisy?" said Skeleton Keys, suddenly looming over them.

"Ugh, this is a private conversation, bone-bag," Daisy huffed. Without pausing, she turned and began walking huffily down the hill.

"Uh, thanks, Daisy!" Stanley called after her. He gazed at her picture of Lucky before looking up at Skeleton Keys. "Does – does Daisy have any friends, Mr Keys?"

"She will, as soon as she decides that she needs them. Until then, she has me," the skeleton replied. "Now, sprout, if I remember rightly, I promised you a long and flabbergasting tale. So then, where to begin...?"

So there we have it, dallywanglers! The truly unbelievable, unbelievably true tale of *The Wild Imaginings of Stanley Strange*. Did I not tell you it was a hum-dum-dinger? Dinosaurs! Robots! Invaders from another imagination! And, of course, the sort of friend that you can only dream of.

Well, 'tis time for Ol' Mr Keys to take his leave – I already feel my remarkable twitch leading me and my partner-in-problem-solving to yet more adventures. Who knows where the twitch will take us? Perhaps to a tale so truly unbelievable that it must, unbelievably, be true. For it has been said, and it cannot be denied, that strange things can happen when imaginations run wild...

Until next time, until next tale, farewell!

Your servant in storytelling,

—SK

BRINGING THE CHARACTERS TO LIFE

Guy and Pete explain how the characters evolved...

Stanley

GB: I wanted Stanley to have a couple of memorable visual elements (glasses and hat) that Lucky could use to describe him. Pete did all the legwork in making him look cool – I didn't even expect him to be on the cover!

PW: Luckily I have quite an impressive collection of spectacles and striped beanie hats, so Stanley's design came quite quickly.

Lucky

GB: In my mind, Lucky looked like a sort of living cartoon character – bright, appealing, larger than life, endlessly wide-eyed and fascinated. The striped pouch was a nod to Pete's love of stripes! Pete did some great sketches and we combined various elements for the final look.

PW: It was exciting to imagine Lucky from Guy's description – the (literally) bouncy character that he described was great fun to create. If there is ever a range of Skeleton Keys toys, I think Lucky might be one of the most popular.

Lady Bryd

GB: Lady Byrd was another character whose look I pictured very clearly, especially the wing casing that folded to form a sort of skirt. I love how she turned out – appealing but still quite unnerving.

PW: Her design involved looking at actual ladybirds, so it was a good opportunity to spend a while wandering around my garden in the sun looking for them. We wanted an elegant, stylish and also 'insecty' character and I think we achieved that.

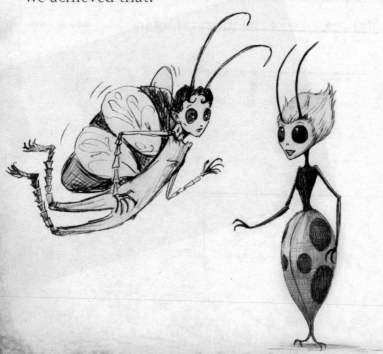

ImagiNathan

GB: I came up with ImagiNathan at around the same time as Skeleton Keys so I was chuffed to be able to put him in a book at last. In the first draft he had a giant forehead but he gradually morphed into a much flashier magician character, coming and going in a puff of smoke.
As frustrating as Skeleton Keys finds him, he is a little jealous of ImagiNathan's showmanship.

PW: I loved trying to capture the swagger that Guy gave to ImagiNathan – and then contrasting it with the more bashed up feeling he had as the story progressed.

Guy Bass is an award-winning author and
semi-professional geek. He has written over thirty books,
including the best-selling *Stitch Head* series (which has been
translated into sixteen languages) *Dinkin Dings and the
Frightening Things* (winner of a 2010 Blue Peter Book Award)
*Spynosaur, Laura Norder: Sheriff of Butts Canyon, Noah Scape
Can't Stop Repeating Himself, Atomic!* and *The Legend of Frog.*

Guy has previously written plays for both adults and children.
He lives in London with his wife and imaginary dog.
Find out more at guybass.com

Pete Williamson is a self-taught artist and illustrator.
He is best known for the much-loved *Stitch Head* series by
Guy Bass, and the award-winning *The Raven Mysteries*
by Marcus Sedgwick.

Pete has illustrated over seventy books by authors including
Francesca Simon, Matt Haig, Steve Cole, Robert Louis
Stevenson and Charles Dickens.

Pete now lives at the very edge of a little town in Kent with
his family, overlooking a field that he has only just found out
might be an ancient burial ground.
Find out more at petewilliamson.co.uk

Have you read *Stitch Head*?

'It's dark, monstrous fun!' Wondrous Reads

In Castle Grotteskew something BIG
is about to happen to someone SMALL.
Join a mad professor's first creation as
he steps out of the shadows into the
adventure of an almost lifetime...

Read all Stitch Head's adventures:

WANT TO FIND

OUT ABOUT

SKELETON KEYS'

OTHER ADVENTURES?

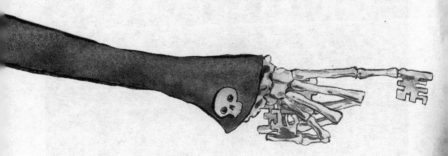

OPEN DOORS TO HIDDEN WORLDS...

SKELETON KEYS

THE UNIMAGINARY FRIEND

WRITTEN BY
GUY BASS

ILLUSTRATED BY
PETE WILLIAMSON

When Ben's imaginary friend, the Gorblimey, suddenly becomes real, Skeleton Keys is convinced the little monster is dangerous. But someone far more monstrous is out there, waiting to take revenge on Ben...

OPEN DOORS TO HIDDEN WORLDS...

SKELETON KEYS

THE HAUNTING OF LUNA MOON

WRITTEN BY
GUY BASS

ILLUSTRATED BY
PETE WILLIAMSON

When Luna's family members start disappearing before her very eyes she thinks her ghostly granddad is to blame. But Skeleton Keys isn't so sure – he's certain something even more mysterious lurks in the shadows – something UNIMAGINARY.

OPEN DOORS TO HIDDEN WORLDS...

SKELETON KEYS

THE LEGEND OF GAP-TOOTH JACK

WRITTEN BY
GUY BASS

ILLUSTRATED BY
PETE WILLIAMSON

When a dangerous UNIMAGINARY escapes into the past, Skeleton Keys must team up with Gap-tooth Jack to thwart its sinister schemes. But there's something about Jack that is strangely familiar...

OPEN DOORS TO HIDDEN WORLDS...

SKELETON KEYS

THE NIGHT OF THE NOBODY

WRITTEN BY
GUY BASS

ILLUSTRATED BY
PETE WILLIAMSON

When shapeless UNIMAGINARY, the Nobody, turns the villagers of Matching Trousers into zombie-like nobodies, not even Skeleton Keys can help. Can Flynn Twist become the hero of his imagination and save the day?